Make Me Stay

Aline Hunter

DEDICATION

To my one and only.
I couldn't do anything without you.

CHAPTER ONE

KAMDEN STONE LAMENTED his lot in life as he drove up the gravel road that would take him to Everly Mason's home. Sundays were meant for rest and relaxation, not menial chores he wasn't in the mood for. He tried to stifle his frustration and resentment. His mother meant well when she did things like this. She wanted him to move on with his life and find happiness and love. She simply didn't understand how circumstances in his life had changed him, removing illusions of grandeur. He took a deep breath, easing off the gas, trying to get his head on straight.

He was who he was.

There was nothing he could do about it.

He made it to the unfinished driveway, parked several feet from the house currently under renovation, and reached for the gloves he'd stashed in the glove compartment. At least he wouldn't be here long. Three frosts had hit the area, so removing the wasp nests wouldn't pose much of an issue. Everly had mentioned her allergy and dilemma when his father had dropped in to check on her. She'd told him she'd take care of them before the spring, but that didn't matter. His father had shared the information with his mother, who informed Kamden he'd better go over as soon as possible to eliminate the issue. He'd put the chore off for a week, gotten calls from his parents to ask if he'd taken care of the problem, and decided it was best to get things over with. He only hoped he could behave himself. The young woman he was about to face had a voice like honey and a smile that made him want to do all sorts of things to her.

He could only handle her in small doses.

Gazing out the window, he looked to see if she or the dogs she cared for were around. His mother indicated she worked with a local rescue, offering pooches sanctuary and care until they were adopted. The front doors to the house and trailer were closed, and he could make out a couple of forms in the large kennels she'd placed between the two. Unable to see anything of importance, he figured she must be working on the house. He shook his head, wondering how the fuck she stayed warm on days like this. Winter weather in Alabama could be the absolute worst. Whereas some days were warm, others were freezing cold. It was unlikely she'd had the heating and air looked at yet.

Tucking the gloves into his coat, he opened the door and climbed out. A gust of biting wind hit him in the face, reminding him that a cold front was moving in. In an effort to stay warm, he closed the door and moved, deciding to check the house first. Midway there, he heard a deep howl coming from within, indicating he'd find the woman he needed to speak with inside. He marched up the stairs, walked over the porch, and to the entrance.

Before he could knock, he heard a soft voice order. "Place."

Shuffling came from inside, followed by purring praise and then soft footsteps. With the click of a lock, the door opened wide, and the woman he'd avoided for weeks appeared right in front of him. She had wood stain on her shirt and overalls. The thin red bandana covering her nose and mouth had seen better days. She'd braided her thick fall of sun-kissed brown hair into two rows that cascaded over her shoulders and tossed on the baseball cap she always wore.

Her hazel eyes were full of confusion as she yanked the bandana down, revealing her pert nose, full lips, and rounded chin. "Kamden?" She shifted to the side so she could look behind him, trying to see if he was alone. Once she knew he'd visited her on his lonesome, her gaze returned to his. "Is everything okay? What are you doing here?"

"Dad said you had some nests you need gone," he informed her, slipping his gloves on. "Take me to them."

Her brows came together and she frowned. "I told him I could handle it."

"Be that as it may," he said, feeling as annoyed as she sounded, "he wants me to help. He won't let me hear the end of it until I do." He lifted his head, meeting her level stare. "Show me where they are and we can both go about our day." Her eyes darkened and her lips thinned, making it apparent she wasn't happy he'd interrupted her. He understood her reaction on numerous levels. He didn't like it when people showed up at his home unannounced. "Look." He lowered his voice, making things clear. "You let me do this, or when he asks if I got this done, I'll have to tell him you told me to leave. Then he'll be paying you another visit to take care of it. He's not as spry as he used to be, and I don't want him climbing on shit if I can help it. Do us both a favor, and show me where they are."

Her hesitation and uncertainty reminded him of their differences. She had to be a decade younger than him, if not more. She was also delicately made and lean as a newborn colt. In contrast, he stood at six foot four inches tall and was built like his father. His size might be intimidating, especially as they were on her property alone. He also didn't know her story or why she'd moved so far into the country, so there could be more to it. They'd only spoken twice, when she'd visited his parent's home, so she didn't know him that well. He'd been polite as his family would kill him otherwise, going through the motions, but he'd been distant and left as soon as he could. There was a good chance she didn't trust him or want him around her. As a single woman living alone, he respected her concern.

After several seconds, she took a step back, giving him room to enter. "They're in the attic."

He waited until she was clear, not wanting to crowd her, and entered the house. To his surprise, she'd accomplished numerous things. The floors had been sanded, stained, and resealed. The walls had also been smoothed out and repainted. She'd even tackled the ceiling. At the moment, she was working on the fireplace. She'd replaced the brick portions with variegated stone, adding an indented area, and was in the middle of refinishing the hearth. His attention landed on the large dog he'd met when he'd cut down a rotting tree on his parent's land. The tricolored animal rested on a bed, mouth open and tag flopping. A couple of kerosene heaters were going, and she had turned on a rotating fan to move air through the room.

She closed the door and faced him. "It's this way."

He didn't tell her he knew the place. The previous resident had been a friend of his parents, so he'd dropped things off here and there when he'd been asked. Frank Wilson had several health issues and hadn't been a neat or tidy person. The last time he'd come inside, the place had been in pretty rough shape. Seeing what she'd done in such a short amount of time was truly impressive.

They made it to the hallway, and she went to retrieve a step ladder. Not wanting to be a complete dick by reminding her he could reach the cord above them, he cleared his throat and stared at her. She looked over her shoulder, saw him in the hallway, and realized what he was trying to communicate. He tugged the panel down, unfolded the stairs, and stepped aside so she could lead the way.

She hurried over and started climbing. "I hope you're not afraid of spiders."

He ignored what she said, moving behind her, when he peered up and got a good look at her ass. *Damn it.* For a trim girl, she certainly had a nice one, all plump and round. The globes shifted from side to side with each step. It took everything in him not to reach out and give one of her cheeks a playful smack.

Don't even fucking go there.

He ripped his eyes from the delectable sight, thinking he needed to get his dick under control, and followed her up. The girl was off-limits. His mother and father would kill him if he treated her like his one-night stands. They'd made it clear how much they liked her, talking about her every chance they could, inviting her over every Sunday. It was the reason his father insisted he get off his ass and help her with the nests in the first place.

He climbed up and noted she'd cleaned everything out. She'd even dusted.

Busy little bee.

He bit back a smile when he realized she'd brought up spiders to be a smart-ass. A few might linger here and there, but there weren't many hiding spots for the ones a person should really worry about. She went to the window and showed him the nests near the ceiling. There were several of them clustered together. By summer, they'd be in bloom. It was a good thing his father was looking out for her.

"I need a garbage bag."

She dug into her pocket and pulled one out. "Here."

"Was all that at the door for show?" He took the plastic bag from her, cocking a brow, teasing her even though a voice in his head said he was treading into dangerous waters.

She stilled, meeting his gaze. "What do you mean?"

"You acted surprised to see me, but you have what I need with you. You were expecting me, weren't you?" He almost grinned when his words landed. She looked stunned and surprised. He didn't stop there, continuing, "You could have made me some coffee to fight the chill. It's cold as hell up here."

"I keep a couple of garbage bags with me at all times. In case you haven't noticed, I'm restoring a house," she replied briskly, placing her hands on her trim hips. "There's coffee in the kitchen if you think you're developing hypothermia. You can get some before you leave."

He picked up what she was putting down. One teasing question and she was on the warpath, hitting him with a solid dose of sarcasm. It didn't take much to rile her up.

Interesting.

The nests were taken care of in seconds. He tied the trash bag off and offered it to her. "There you go, ma'am." This time he didn't wait for her to go first. Seeing the fire in her eyes, watching as she'd confronted him without a care in the world, had him wondering how she'd feel against him if he pinned her to the wall. He forced aside the tempting image, fully aware he didn't need to go there. "Consider me out of your hair."

He went down the stairs and reached for his phone. His mother had invited him over for lunch, but he was about to decline the offer. He was going home, taking a shower, and venturing into town. Chris, his friend and employee, had been asking him to shoot some pool the last couple of weeks. They could enjoy a game and have a few drinks. If he was lucky, Charlene would be around. She'd had a bitch of a breakup and shared his sentiments about relationships. They hooked up from time to time, taking advantage of no-strings sex that pleased them both.

The loud snap of wood giving way caught his attention.

As he turned, he noticed Everly's right ankle twist

awkwardly as the step gave way. His stomach knotted, his heart lodging in his throat. He wasn't close enough to catch her, only able to rush to her. She met his gaze, her bright eyes growing wide, and lost her balance. She tripped over the remaining stairs, dropping the garbage bag, and cried out as the cap flew from her head. She fell a couple of feet and landed on the ground with a loud thump. The dog barked, and he heard nails darting across the floor. It ran to her, tail wagging, trying to lick her face.

Going to her, he gently pushed the dog aside and knelt. "Are you all right?" She shook her head, holding the ankle that had taken the bad turn. "Let me see." He didn't wait for permission, moving her hands aside. The minute he tried to move it, testing for breaks, she hissed and grasped his arm.

"Don't move it," she said, in obvious pain. "God, that hurts."

The dog went back at her, nearly knocking her over. He was about to remove the beast when she intervened. "It's okay, Baloo." She snapped her fingers and pointed at the living room. "Place." The animal didn't listen, and she repeated the instruction, her voice more commanding. "Place."

Baloo whined but left them, doing as he'd been told.

"How bad does it look?" She groaned and squirmed when he applied a bit of pressure around the bone. "Do you think it's broken?"

He didn't move her ankle, but he did touch it with caution. He bit back a curse when he noticed it had already started swelling. The only way to know the amount of damage was to take her to the nearest emergency clinic.

"I'm not sure. You need to get an x-ray." He went to work untying her shoe. The high-top converse might be difficult to remove if the inflammation increased. "Family Care is open. They can transfer you if you need to go to the hospital."

She shifted her body, ready to get up. "I don't have time for this."

"Nuh-uh. Don't even try it." He wasn't overly forceful, placing a hand on her thigh, but he wouldn't let her put weight on the injury. She had to have it looked at whether she liked it or not. "Do you have any furniture in this place?"

Her eyes darted from her ankle, and their gazes met and held. This was the first time he'd seen her without a baseball cap. Without one, he got an unhindered look at her face. She was more than attractive; the woman was fucking gorgeous. Her brows were perfectly arched, bringing attention to her eyes. This close, almost face-to-face with her, he noted her irises consisted of brown in the center and grey along the rim.

"The kitchen," she answered softly, bringing him back to himself.

He slid his hand under her knees and placed another at her back. "Put your arms around my neck."

When she didn't comply, he figured to hell with it. He could lift her without her holding on. He stood, and she quickly looped her right arm around him like he'd asked. She weighed less than a mite, easy enough to tote around. He tried not to think about how good she felt against him as he went into the kitchen, spotted a small table and two chairs, and took her to the furniture.

"I'll put out the heaters. Are there any other things that need to be shut down?" She shook her head. Recalling what she'd said about coffee, he asked, "Where's the coffee pot?"

"Thermos," she corrected. "It's on the counter."

"I'll be right back." He left her to get things done, wanting to get her to the clinic. If she'd broken her ankle, he wasn't sure what she'd do. She'd chosen to live alone, in the middle of fucking nowhere, with nothing but a ragtag group of dogs. He hadn't seen family or friends visit, meaning she didn't have someone nearby to care for her.

He grimaced when he considered that.

His parents would lap this up. They'd send him to her home on the daily. Hell, they'd probably ask him to work on her house while she recovered since he had the knowledge and tools to do it. The more time he spent with her, the more he'd want her. Like he wasn't already suffering from that malady. One minute in her presence was one minute too long.

He knew he shouldn't have come to her home.

Fuck.

Everly leaned over, cursing her shitty luck, studying her ankle. She'd almost finished her task for the week. Due to this, her schedule would be all over the place. She wanted to be out of the crappy trailer by the spring. By the looks of things, it might be the summer. Since the mobile home didn't have air conditioning, she'd swelter.

She heard Kamden moving around stilled.

The man confused the hell out of her.

He hadn't been rude the first time they'd been introduced, but he hadn't exactly been nice. She got the feeling he didn't want to be anywhere near her. The second time was much like the first, only when he'd walked in and found her chatting with his mother, he'd turned to leave without greeting either of them. His mother had seen him, however, and reprimanded him for his behavior. He'd entered the living room, slapping on a smile faker than silicone, and talked to them for a couple of minutes. Even then, she'd gotten an odd vibe from him, like she was something he needed to avoid.

For that reason, she'd been stunned when she'd answered the door and found him standing on her porch.

He hadn't dressed up, wearing a logo T-shirt, faded blue jeans, scuffed boots, and a heavy jacket, but he'd taken the time to style his hair and trim the whiskers on his face. His eyes were the color of whiskey surrounded by firelight, a brown that appeared almost gold. He was unfairly good-looking, both tall and muscular, and she thought he knew it. That only made her angry and bitter, as he'd shown no interest in her.

Then he'd talked to her in the attic, taking her completely off guard. He'd actually appeared to be flirting. It was the first time he'd acted like she didn't have the plague.

His mood swings didn't make any sense whatsoever.

Maybe he has a chemical imbalance.

She heard footsteps coming toward the kitchen and sat up.

He came around the corner, holding the coat she'd placed on the hanger beside the front door. "What about the dog?"

Baloo was her personal dog, not one of her fosters, so she knew he wouldn't get into things or use the house as his toilet. Since she'd put in a doggie door, he could let himself out and go to the backyard if necessary. She'd have preferred to take him with her, but she didn't think the clinic would allow him inside.

Let's get this over with.

"He'll be fine here." She took the coat when he offered it to her, slid her arms into it, and motioned to the counter. "Will you hand me my backpack?"

He snagged it with his right hand and brought it over. She unzipped the front pocket and pulled out her keys. "Can you help me to my car?"

"Your car?" The way he said it forced her eyes from the keys. He was frowning, looking at her like she'd lost her mind. "You're not driving."

Like hell I'm not. "I'm capable of getting myself to the

clinic."

"You aren't driving," he repeated. He took the backpack and slid it over his shoulder. "I'll take you."

Her temper sparked. "Why would you want to?"

"What's that supposed to mean?"

"It means what it means." Her ankle was throbbing, and she was beyond caring if she sounded like a bitch. She didn't know why he acted like he did, but she'd had enough. She met his glaring eyes, making sure they looked right at each other when she told him the truth. "It's obvious you don't like being anywhere near me. Why torture yourself?"

His expression changed, indicating he hadn't expected the response. "That's not true."

"Bullshit." She had toxic family members. Over the years, she'd gotten good at reading people. It was one of the reasons she stopped visiting Kamden's parents. As nice as they were, and as much as she enjoyed being around them, she didn't like being treated like a pariah by their son. "Every time you see me, you act like a natural disaster is on the way. The first time I thought it was me. I knew it was all on you the second time. I don't know what your deal is, but I'm not in the mood for your flakiness. I don't spend time with people who treat me like crap. Life's too short."

Silence hovered between them. His eyes changed, becoming almost haunted. She thought her declaration had wounded him somehow, which made her feel like shit. She wasn't the kind of person who enjoyed other people's suffering. He didn't owe her anything. She didn't have a right to put him in his place or talk down to him.

"It's not what you think," he replied quietly, holding her stare.

"It doesn't matter." She severed eye contact and rattled her keys, ready to stand up and hop out of the house if she had to. "Are you going to help me to my car or not?"

"Everly, darlin'," he said, his voice a low growl that had her chin flying right back up. When their gazes met this time, he didn't look disinterested. In fact, he was looking at her in a way that made her insides melt. He came toward her slowly, each movement slow and deliberate. He brought his hand down, took her keys, and informed her in a deep voice, "I'm driving you to the clinic. End of discussion."

He reached for her, but she stopped him.

"Baloo," she called out, wanting to see him before she left. Her father had given her the Greater Swiss Mountain Dog four years ago, and she didn't go anywhere without the pup. He rushed into the kitchen, happy to be called, coming straight to her. She placed her fingers behind his ears and scratched them for a few seconds. Then she lowered her face and rested it against his broad head. "I have to go for a little while. You be good, okay? Wait here for me." After giving him a quick kiss on the muzzle, she said, "Hold the fort. I'll be back soon."

Lowering her hands, she noticed Kamden watching her.

The heat in his eyes had been replaced with something she couldn't identify. That wasn't new when it came to the man. She had no idea what was going on in that head of his. She tried not to be self-conscious, sick and tired of trying to figure out what it was about her that caused him to behave so oddly. She'd never had a problem attracting men, and she didn't want to keep dissecting herself to figure out what he did and didn't like about her.

"All set?"

She nodded, ready to stand and hobble to the car with his help when he extended his arms and indicated he intended to carry her. She almost declined the offer, recalling how good he smelled when he'd brought her into the kitchen but decided to let him have his way. The sooner she got her ankle looked at, the sooner she could get back home. She wrapped her hands around his neck, and he lifted her like she weighed next to nothing. The instant she felt his muscular form against her, the desire she'd kept in check came to life. She moved her ankle, clenching her teeth, using pain to keep lusty feelings away. Other men might find her alluring, but this one certainly didn't.

They made it to the door, and he locked up.

As he carried her to his truck, she said a silent prayer that nothing else would spring up and bite her in the ass. It didn't look like she was on the good side of lady luck, and the day had only just begun.

CHAPTER TWO

KAMDEN SAT IN the waiting area, staring at the television mounted in the corner, wondering how much longer Everly would be in the back. Two hours had gone by, and several people had entered and left. He didn't think she'd be making a trip to the hospital. The doctor would have made that decision after viewing the x-rays. He wondered how severe the injury was, hoping it was something she'd overcome with a minimal recovery period. Judging from the work she'd done on the house, she liked to stay busy. He didn't think she'd do well if she had to be off her feet for more than a couple of weeks.

He hadn't spoken to her on the drive to the clinic, trying to put his head on straight. His thoughts drifted, taking him back to her kitchen. He thought he'd been polite and a complete gentleman in their previous encounters but, judging by the cold look in her eyes and the way she'd addressed him, he'd been mistaken. She'd not only seen right through him, she'd called him out on his bullshit. He hadn't meant to hurt her. Hell, he'd only spoken to her the two times. He hadn't willingly engaged in conversation or idle chatter, but he'd made sure to treat her as courteously as possible.

At least, he thought he had.

What the hell did he do now? Tell her that he didn't do relationships? Explain that the only woman he'd ever loved decided to fuck around with his best friend? Would she understand how something like that changed a person? Even if she did, would it really matter?

They hardly knew each other.

If she hadn't taken a nasty fall, he'd have left her place and gone about his business. Sure, he'd have thought about her. In the last few weeks, it seemed she was constantly on his mind. That was why he tried to stay away from her. He hoped his curiosity would go away. If he'd managed to leave as soon as he'd removed the nests in the attic, they wouldn't have seen each other unless they accidentally crossed paths or she accepted an invitation to Sunday dinner with his folks.

That line of thinking brought him back to the present.

She thought he didn't like being around her, and she was right. Trouble was, she thought it was because he didn't like her. In that, she was very wrong.

The first time he'd been introduced—as soon as she'd told him hello with her sultry voice and revealed her impish smile—he felt a stirring inside him he hadn't experienced since his first love, Delaney. Everly was the kind of woman that had a man thinking about more than sex. Only a fool wouldn't consider long-term possibilities. Not only was she beautiful, she cared about other people. He'd known that when he saw how she treated his parents. For fuck's sake, just watching her with her dog had melted his heart. She touched the large animal with reverence and spoke to it with complete adoration. When she'd brought her forehead down and rested it on the beast's head, treating it like a beloved family member, he knew why she fostered dogs in the first place. Not only did she love them, she needed them as much as they needed her.

Everly Mason, despite her happy-go-lucky attitude, was lonely.

He hadn't expected that, and it bothered the hell out of him.

21

So what to do?

He considered telling her the truth and asking if they could be friends. It would be difficult, as she was tempting as sin, but he could keep a leash on himself. If they came to some kind of understanding, she'd be able to visit his family more often. He could also drive over to her place a couple of times a week to see how she was getting along. She'd have someone to talk to, which might ease the sadness within her. Despite his fucked up history, he didn't like to see a woman upset or in need of something. He made sure to be crystal clear with those he fooled around with, ensuring they knew things wouldn't go anywhere with him. There was always an understanding before any deviousness took place. He didn't want to break anyone's heart.

He knew how shitty that kind of thing felt.

He heard the door to the back area opening and lifted his head. Everly appeared, moving slowly, trying to adjust the crutches under her arms and the boot on her left foot. She gazed around, spotted him, and cautiously started in his direction. The coat got in her way, as did the backpack. She scowled and stopped to move things around, struggling with the braids that also got in her way. He stood and made it to her in three long strides, making sure she didn't go anywhere.

"Give me that." He reached for the backpack, wanting the fucking thing out of her way before she hurt herself again.

"I've got it," she grumbled.

"I said"—he reached out and grasped the bag—"give it to me."

She narrowed her eyes, passed it to him, and he asked, "How bad is it?"

"A bad sprain, but nothing's broken."

Thank God. "How's the pain?"

"They iced it, so it's bearable. I'm supposed to repeat

that and keep it elevated as much as possible." She shifted her arms, trying to get comfortable in the crutches. "The doctor wrote me a prescription."

He wanted to snatch the crutches and carry her out, but he didn't think she'd appreciate it. During the drive to the clinic, he wasn't the only one who'd remained silent. She hadn't said a word, staring out the window, resting her head against the seat. He wanted to know what was on her mind, but he'd been afraid to ask. As much as he dreaded it, they had to have a conversation. She'd called him out, and she had every right to do so. He wouldn't leave things like this. He simply didn't know what he'd say.

"I'll take you to Marshall's Pharmacy, and we can wait at Penny's while the prescription is filled." They could get her medication and eat at the cafe next door. During that time, he'd try to figure out how to talk to her. "Is that all right with you?" When she didn't respond, not meeting his eyes, he chose to be honest with her for the first time. "I've been an ass, but you're wrong about one thing. It's not because I don't want to be around you." He waited until she met his gaze before he told her, "The truth is, I've acted like a prick because I'd like to be around you in a way you probably wouldn't be comfortable with."

Her eyes widened, revealing she hadn't expected him to say something so blunt and to the point. Before she could respond, a couple came through the automatic doors behind them. The pair skirted around them, going to the counter to sign in. They couldn't have a discussion here. The waiting room was quiet, and he didn't want anyone listening in. To say what he wanted, they needed some kind of privacy. He went to her side, ready to grab her if she stumbled.

"Can I take you to Marshall's?" he asked, giving her the opportunity to tell him to fuck off.

"Okay," she responded, sounding somewhat awestruck.

He remained beside her as they made the trek to his truck, trying to think ahead. Honesty was probably best in this situation. His neutral responses had obviously upset her, and he didn't want that. Unfortunately, the idea of telling her the truth made him nauseous. He'd avoided this topic with his family, wanting to maneuver around it, aware a discussion would take him back to life-altering instances he wanted to forget.

They made it to the passenger side of the truck. She stumbled, struggling with the crutches. He was right there, moving behind her, latching on to her waist. He pulled her back, resting his hand against her soft belly, keeping her upright. He almost groaned, finding that she was the perfect fit for him. She drew a ragged breath like the close contact affected her as much as it did him.

He couldn't prevent his natural reaction, aware of the pulse in his cock as blood flowed to the organ, hardening it in a way that made him want to reach down to shift himself in his jeans. He moved his hips slightly, not wanting her to feel his physical response, and pressed the button on his keychain to unlock the vehicle. He reached around her, opening her door, wanting her to get in the truck before he turned her around and kissed her long and hard.

He used his free hand to collect the crutches.

"In you go," he said, wincing when he heard how deep his voice had become.

He took her off her feet with the surrounding arm, taking another step toward the truck so she could climb inside. She grasped the roof handle, rotated her hips, and sank into the seat. He let her go and took care as he placed his hand under her injured foot, helping her place it on the floorboard. With that done, he removed her backpack and placed it in her lap. When he lifted his head, wanting to see her, he found her focus was already on him. She didn't say anything, simply watched him.

He saw something he didn't expect in her gaze.

Curiosity, excitement, and expectation.

He immediately looked away, making sure she was clear before closing the door. He tossed the crutches into the back of the truck and took deep breaths as he went around the vehicle. He reminded himself that she was young and wasn't prepared for someone like him. He liked his sex hard and rough. He also had a foul mouth when he got down and dirty. He'd say things that would probably offend her. He wasn't easy to be with, working long hours, wanting to be the provider, expecting his woman to be at home when he walked through the door with dinner on the table. Delaney hadn't liked that, telling him to join the rest of society in the 21st century.

Then there was his possessive nature.

When he'd found Josh with Delaney having sex in his bed, he'd been stunned. He'd known Josh since he was a kid and had started dating Delaney when he was sixteen. Something in his mind clicked, and he'd realized he wasn't with his friend and girlfriend anymore. She'd been riding his Josh like a pony, making all kinds of noises. It had taken all of his control not to kill the man who'd touched what was his. He'd wanted to rip the son of a bitch apart, even though the woman he loved had taken part in the transgression of her own free will. At that moment, he'd been so broken up, he wanted to believe his friend had been taking advantage. He'd pummeled the hell out of Josh, breaking his former friend's nose in the process, until his anger ebbed and he could think clearly. He still wasn't sure how he'd remained calm afterward, addressing the two of them like children, telling them to get out of his home. They'd tried to explain and offer excuses, but he hadn't wanted to hear any of it, repeating the same thing over and over.

"Get the fuck out."

He didn't open his door for several seconds, trapped in

vile memories that tormented him for years, not willing to chance another repeat. Recalling the event, reminded of the scent of sex drifting into his nostrils when he'd found them, he remembered he wasn't in the past anymore. He glanced through the window, finding Everly had watched him as he'd journeyed around the truck. Her hazel eyes rested on him, revealing a willingness to accept what she didn't yet understand. She was too good for him. Too pure. Shaking his head, trying to collect himself, he reached for the handle and prepared to climb into the cabin.

Everly wasn't Delaney.

It wasn't fair to lash out at her for something she hadn't done.

As he slid into his seat and put the keys in the ignition, he acknowledged he had to come clean. The girl next to him had to understand he hadn't always been a deplorable bastard. He'd held on to his resentment for nearly a decade. His mother, father, and even his brother had urged him to move on. He might be taking a risk in opening himself to a woman again, but he hoped the effort would be worth it.

He'd avoided her for one reason.

She made him want things he thought he'd never have.

CHAPTER THREE

WHAT THE HELL is going on?

First, Kamden acted disinterested. Now he wanted to take her to Penny's Cafe to explain himself. He'd told her he'd like to be around her in a way she wouldn't be comfortable with. If he meant what she thought he did, he'd be wrong. The moment she'd been introduced to Kamden, she'd felt an instant attraction. That was the reason his dismissal hurt so much. She knew the effect she had on the opposite sex. She'd only dated two men, but she'd been asked out numerous times. He was the first man she'd been attracted to on sight. To have him turn away from her, treating her like some foul creature, had destroyed her confidence.

She checked her watch. It was almost three o'clock in the afternoon. "I need to be home by five," she said quietly, releasing her coat, settling back in the seat.

Kamden glanced at her. "Why five?"

"I called the rescue after the doctor told me to stay off my feet." The call hadn't been easy to make. By moving the dogs she'd been caring for, she'd limit space in other homes. The less space, the fewer that could be pulled from the pound. "They're sending someone to take my fosters."

"You don't sound happy about it."

That was an understatement. "Because I'm not."

He peered over at her again. "Anything I can do?"

Her eyes drifted over as she braced herself, thinking

he'd be a smart-ass. Their gazes met, and she softened, seeing the compassion in his golden gaze. He wasn't offering because he felt he had to. He actually wanted to help.

"No," she answered, giving him a small smile. "They require a lot of time and exercise."

"Do I look out of shape to you?" He shifted his attention back to the road.

No, he certainly did not. He had the musculature of a man who did physical labor each day. She'd learned he was a project manager in a construction business, so it made sense. "That's not the issue. One is still a puppy. I have to get up a couple of times a night to let him out."

He kept watching the road, not looking at her. "Are you asking me to stay at your place?"

That made her laugh. Until the house was ready, she had to live in the mobile home that didn't have a bit of space and was on its last wheel. "Have you seen my trailer?"

His jaw clenched as though he didn't like thinking about it. "I don't understand why you stay there. You could rent a refurbished one while you work on the house."

"It's not that bad. I'll be able to move out of it this summer. I'm not throwing away money to live in comfort for a few months."

"Living on a budget?"

It was a trick question, and she knew it. He wanted to know how she made a living. She wasn't surprised. She'd moved to the property and didn't leave it unless she had to buy food or essentials. He had to know she didn't have a job in town. Since she wasn't of retirement age, he likely wanted to know how she'd made such a thing possible. If the roles were reversed, she'd be curious too.

"An extremely tight budget," she admitted. If she watched her finances closely, she could live comfortably for the rest of her life. Kamden shot her a confounded look, and she spilled the tea. "My dad died a few months ago. He left me some money and the property. The house and land belonged to his grandparents. We moved around a lot and weren't going to use it, so he rented it out for extra income."

"I'm sorry."

"Don't be. Dad didn't want anyone to be upset when he was gone. He made me promise I would move on with my life. He said he'd haunt me if I didn't live life to the fullest."

"Sounds like he was a smart man."

He'd been far more than that. "He was."

His lips curved at the corners. "You're an heiress?"

"I've never really thought about it like that." She'd been given a lot, but she wasn't exactly rich. "I suppose I am if there's a Dollar General variety."

He chuckled. "Is he the one who taught you how to restore houses?"

"He was."

Her old man hadn't liked her interest in the flipping business, but once she'd made up her mind, there was no stopping her. He'd finally caved, showing her the tricks of the trade. She'd spent every free moment working with him, finding the sense of accomplishment did more for her than spending a day with friends. Her father had always told her she was an old soul.

"That's what he did for a living?"

"Not early on." They'd struggled when she'd been little. She remembered those days vividly. He'd hated putting her in daycare, but he hadn't been given any other choice. They both had to make sacrifices for the greater good. "It took a few years. He had to save up first."

"What about your mom?"

He'd asked the one question she wasn't ready to answer. Rotating in her seat to face him, she switched things up. "Nope. It's my turn." She noted him gripping the steering wheel, seeming to brace himself for all-out war. "What is it about me you don't like?"

Why have you always treated me like cancer?

"I already told you," he said slowly. "It's not what you think."

"And what do I think?" Maybe if she knew that much, she would understand.

He didn't answer right away, turning on the road that would take them to the cafe. She worried she'd over-played her hand, pushing him to tell her something he wasn't ready to share. A part of her hoped that wasn't the case. Each time they'd spoken, she'd found herself enam-ored with the man. She didn't want him to turn away now that they were actually speaking to each other.

"How old are you, Everly?"

Relief coursed through her. Was that the problem? She did look young for her age. She'd been told she'd appre-ciate that later in life. Did he think she was too young for him? If that was the issue, she could ease his concern. She was definitely of legal age.

"Twenty-two. I'll be twenty-three in March."

"I'm thirty-four." He made it sound like a bad thing.

She figured as much, although he could shave a cou-ple of years and pass himself off as a younger man if he wanted to. "So?"

The response surprised him. "That doesn't bother you?"

The men she'd dated had been in their early twenties, and they hadn't left behind good impressions. Both had wanted to go to parties, hang out with their friends, and play video games. They were also complete slobs who lived off their parents, worked part-time jobs, and were lazy as hell. The only time they spent alone with her involved sex that, most of the time, didn't do anything for her. It was the reason she'd broken up with both of them within a year.

"No," she answered firmly, meaning it, "it doesn't."

He took that in, clutching the steering wheel. "It should bother you, darlin'."

It was the second time he'd called her that, meaning he had to have some kind of interest in her. For some reason, he didn't want to let things happen as they should, keeping himself distant and apart. She didn't know why, but she wasn't going to let him dodge her anymore.

"Don't tell me what should and shouldn't bother me. I'm a big girl, and I can make up my own mind. If that's the problem, I can tell you the age difference doesn't matter to me. It's just a number."

"You also don't know anything about me."

That much was true, but she wanted to. "Then tell me all about you."

His gaze darted to her, his fingers gripping the wheel tighter. "I'm not sure I should."

"You don't sprout fur and howl at the moon once a month, do you? Or go around drinking people's blood? If not, I think I'm good." Her attempt at humor worked. She could see him trying not to grin. "I don't frighten easily."

"I don't do that, but I can be beastly on occasion."

She was about to ask for details when he pulled into the lot, taking up a parking space in front of the pharmacy. He put the truck in park, staring straight ahead, and the tension between them returned. From her vantage point, he looked like he had a lot on his mind. A part of her wanted to reach out, touch him, and tell him he could trust her. Something had happened to him—an event that had changed him—and she needed to know what it was if she wanted to get through to him.

"You wanted to bring me here, right? Things will stay like this unless you talk to me." When he didn't say anything, she took a chance. She reached out and placed her fingers on his forearm. His head turned, his eyes resting on her hand, then slowly inched up. She met his gaze, determined and unafraid. "I want you to talk to me. I want to understand." Because she felt like he needed to hear it, she told him, "You don't know me either, but when you do, you'll find out you can trust me."

Slowly, as though pained, he released the steering wheel and rested his hand over hers. She tried to place the look in his eyes, needing to figure out what had fucked him up so badly. He was a good man. She'd learned that while visiting his parents. They told her he could have moved away a long time ago, going to live with his brother in Tennessee, but decided to build a small house on the opposite side of their property. He lived nearby to watch over them, always ready to make their lives easier, visiting them often to make sure they were taken care of.

He gazed down at their hands, brushed his thumb over her knuckles, and then his golden-brown eyes returned to her face. She wanted to crawl over, climb into his lap, and twine her fingers in his hair.

"We'll talk in Penny's," he said softly.

God help her. She'd never desired a man more.

She wanted to know him inside and out.

"Promise?" she asked, hoping she wouldn't scare him away.

His lips parted, and he almost responded.

Then he looked away and nodded.

She let him go, sliding her hand from his warm fingers and reached for her backpack to remove the prescription she needed to fill. She wanted to understand the man who'd been on her mind for weeks. She'd thought about him each time she studied the outline of his parent's house in the distance, hoping to catch a glimpse of him each time he visited his family.

She'd been captivated the minute she'd spoken to him.

If he was willing to reveal himself, she was more than ready to listen.

The pharmacy hadn't been crowded. Since it was past the afternoon rush, Penny's wasn't bad either. He knew the staff, so it wasn't difficult to get a table in the back near the window. He got Everly situated, pulling up a chair to elevate her foot, and placed her bag and crutches beside her.

Then, slowly, he settled in the seat across from her.

He wasn't sure where the fuck to start. Her response when he'd brought up their age difference, as well as the way she'd gazed at him, made it clear she was interested in him. Had she always been? Had he missed it because he'd spent as little time with her as possible? Neither of those things mattered now, not with her sitting directly in front of him.

"You wouldn't be happy with someone like me," he eventually stated, confessing something that wasn't as hard but nonetheless true.

Her hazel eyes darted from the menu she'd picked up. "Why?"

Thinking it was best, he summed things up. "I'm possessive, bossy, and will want all of your free time."

She absorbed the information and met his gaze. "So? I'm possessive, bossy, and will want all of your free time."

For fuck's sake, did she think this was a game? "I'm not joking."

She didn't back down, smiling slyly. "Neither am I."

The waitress came over, one he'd spoken to more than once, holding a pen and order pad in her hands. He said a prayer, hoping Sheila didn't ruin everything by flirting or getting confrontational. She was aware he wasn't inter ested, but that had never stopped her before. The busty redhead had passed her number along with his orders since they'd met. She'd even called him a few times to tell him when his orders were ready to be picked up.

"Hey, Kamden. Long time no see," she addressed him with a seductive smile, shifting her hips as she moved closer to him. "Are you ready to order?"

"I'm not sure about him," Everly stated, butting right in, "but I am." She didn't wait for Sheila to address her. "I'll have the vegetable soup and sweet tea. Are the crackers in pouches?"

"Yes, they are," Shelia answered, slitting her eyes, openly abrasive. "Why?"

"Just curious," Everly replied, not taking the bait, her own reply saccharine sweet. "I'd also like extra crackers."

Sheila didn't like being challenged. He'd discovered that a couple of months ago. When he'd come inside to pick up his order, a new waitress tried to check him out and collect payment. Shelia had immediately taken over, shoving the young lady aside, offering him a slice of pie for free.

Only she hadn't been offering him food. Not really.

"Will you need separate checks?"

"That won't be necessary," Everly said, placing the menu in the rack next to the condiments. "He asked me here, so he's buying."

Well, hell. The sexy woman across from him wasn't joking. When she said she was possessive as well, she meant it. She'd thrown down the gauntlet without trying. He glanced at Shelia, not making eye contact, hoping she'd get the drift when he said, "I'll have the same, only with coffee instead of tea."

Shelia didn't make things easy, expecting an answer from him. "So one check?"

For some reason, the question pissed him off. He lifted his head and met Sheila's infuriated gaze. "You heard her."

Since he'd never been anything but polite, trying to a gentleman, he caught the waitress off guard. She immediately lowered her eyes, fisting the pad and pen in her hands.

"I'll put in your order."

She pivoted and left them in a hurry.

"It's a good thing I ordered extra crackers," Everly said with laughter in her voice. He gazed at her, curious about what she meant, and she was grinning. "My first job was in fast food, and I just broke a huge rule. Don't ever fuck with people who handle your food. When the soup comes, don't touch it. She'll spit in it if she gets a chance."

"You're a ballsy little thing." He liked that about her.

She shrugged. "Only when someone needs to be put in their proper place. So..." Still watching him, becoming serious, she said, "I can handle possessive, bossy, and I don't mind giving you my free time. That's not the problem, though, is it? There's something else bothering you."

After seeing her talk Sheila down, it was difficult to think. But there was something he wanted to know. "Do you always come on this strong with men you're attracted to?"

"Believe it or not, this is a first." The question didn't faze her. He was beginning to think that not much did. "I've never had to chase anyone, so this is new to me."

With the way she handled herself, he wasn't sure he believed her. "You've never gone after a man before?"

"I've never had to. I've been in two relationships, and both were instigated by the guys. Neither of them worked out."

"Why not?"

"They didn't care about me. Not in the way I wanted them to."

"So you're hoping I'll be different?"

"That goes without saying." Her eyes darkened, and she turned reflective. "Maybe it's stupid on my part, but

I've wanted to know why you ran the first time I met you. It bothers me."

"I didn't run," he corrected. "I did the right thing and got out of your way."

"Because you're bad for me?"

That was one reason. "I'm not an easy man to be with, Everly."

"What makes you say that?"

He glanced behind him and looked around, making sure everyone else was out of earshot. The truth wasn't something he wanted everyone to know. "I'm a Neanderthal and wired like my Dad. I've only been in one relationship, and it ended badly."

Her hazel gaze was full of understanding. "Define badly."

How did he describe having his heart ripped out?

"It started when I was sixteen and ended when I was twenty-three." He'd been stupid back then, thinking they'd be the high school sweethearts who married and stayed together until they died. "She told me I prevented her from having a life of her own, and she wasn't wrong in saying it. I wanted her to stay home while I took care of her. It wasn't easy, but I got us a place and made it work. Like I said, I'm a lot like Dad. You've visited my folks. You know how it is with them."

"She broke up with you because you wanted to be the provider?"

"I broke up with her, actually."

"Oh God," Everly said, revealing how perceptive she could be, figuring out what he hadn't wanted to say. "Did she cheat on you?"

"That she did. With my best friend."

"What an asshole." She paused and her breathing changed. "What a bitch." The venom in her voice shocked him. When he looked at her eyes, the brown in her irises was almost gone, leaving only silver and gold.

"Did she know what you wanted from the start? Did you make it clear?"

That right there was an enormous part of the problem. "She knew. She was attracted to the idea in high school. When we were in college, she changed her mind. She didn't like being tied down and wanted her own social life."

"Wait a minute, hold up." She scowled when she tried to get closer to the table and had to reposition her leg. After a few seconds, she got situated and rested her arms on the table. "You're blaming yourself because she changed?"

"Not blaming myself. Only being honest since you asked."

"No, you're blaming yourself, and you shouldn't be. She made a decision that messed things up, not you. You said she knew how things would be, and she was fine with it. If she had an issue, she should have sat you down and talked to you." Her expression changed, becoming hostile. "I can forgive certain people for cheating because everyone makes mistakes, but on the whole, I can't stand them."

He'd noted her reaction when he'd asked about her mother. There had to be a reason she didn't want to talk about her. "Like your mom?"

Her eyes flared. Disdain and outrage changed her face. He thought she might not answer. She took a deep breath, severing eye contact, staring at the table. "She left Dad and me when I was a baby. She met someone else, married him, and took off."

Suddenly his history didn't seem all that bad. He couldn't imagine what his life would have been like if his parents weren't together. He felt like shit for bringing it up. "I'm sorry." He meant it, too. He couldn't imagine her pain. "I shouldn't have asked."

"I told you because I wanted to. I came with you today

because I wanted to." She hesitated, her gaze flickering to his face. Then she brought her hand over, resting her fingers over his wrist. "No one forced me to be here."

She might not have gone after men before, but she knew how to get the job done. The wall he'd erected around himself started falling, tumbling down one heartache at a time. Even as he felt the shift, he didn't want to give her his heart. If he kept that part of himself out of the equation, he could leave without emotional scars when things turned sour. Despite that, he placed his hand over hers, wanting to touch her. He noted she kept her nails trimmed and tidy but didn't bother with polish. She was a beautiful girl who liked to keep things simple.

"I see why your parents worry about you," she whispered. "No wonder you don't want to meet someone and settle down."

"They told you that, did they?" He wasn't surprised. They'd started setting him up on dates as soon as he turned thirty.

"Actually, no. I didn't ask, and they didn't tell. I figured it out just now."

"If you have it all sorted, what is it you want, Everly Mason?" Maybe it was wrong to ask, but he had no idea what she was up to.

"The same as you, I suppose." Their gazes met and held. "A chance to find a certain someone and be happy."

Before he could respond, a party of five were seated at the large table across from them. God, he had the worst luck sometimes. The timing wasn't good, but there wasn't anything he could do about that. He still had to take her home, so they could speak privately later. She said she wanted a chance to find someone and be happy, and he was starting to believe that wasn't such a bad idea. Thus far, she'd been nothing but honest, listening without interrupting, withholding any judgment.

A different waitress approached, carrying a tray with

their food. They were forced to release each other as she placed their orders in front of them. The woman had a knowing smile on her face like she knew Shelia had been knocked down a peg or two. She asked if she could get them anything else, waited until they told her they were set, and walked away with a bounce in her step.

Everly didn't touch her soup, sliding it to the side and reaching for her backpack. She unzipped it and removed a large bottle of water. Since he didn't want to eat spit, he did the same. He hesitated when he went for the coffee, wondering if that was tainted too.

"You'll usually be able to tell if that's been messed with. You should see foam on the top." Everly collected a cracker and broke it in half. "If you're worried, get a new cup. Tell the waitress it tastes funny." She plopped the bottle of water on the table. "Or we can share this if you want. I don't have cooties."

Now he knew why the backpack was so heavy. "Do you always carry water with you?"

"Sure do. There are snacks in there, too, if you want to take a look. I never know what I'll need or when I'll need it. It's why I don't carry a purse." She took a bite of the cracker and chewed slowly, without a care in the world.

Who is *this woman?*

He knew one thing for sure.

He had to find out.

CHAPTER FOUR

THEY MADE IT back before five, and Everly couldn't believe that things appeared to be different between them. He decided against eating, simply taking the time to get to know her, stroking his thumb over her knuckles. His fingers were calloused, his grip firm. He was gentle as he touched her, treating her like something delicate. He turned out to be something else as well—a complete gentleman. After they'd finished lunch, he'd helped her get up, took her to get her pain medication, and stayed close so she wouldn't trip over things or fall. She couldn't fathom anyone cheating on him.

His ex-girlfriend had to be completely insane.

They hit the drive to her house, and she gazed at him. He looked more relaxed, the fine lines around his lips and eyes completely smoothed out. Now that she understood him better, she wanted to spend more time with him. He still had his guard up, but he wasn't cold or distant any longer.

Given an opportunity, she believed she could get through to him.

She spotted a red Ford Bronco in front of the house and stifled a wince. She'd been told someone would retrieve the dogs, but she hadn't expected the person to be Brett. He was the primary veterinarian at the rescue and often went out of his way to help. He flirted with her here and there, calling a few times a week, encouraging her to accept his offer to take her to dinner. He'd made his interest obvious, and everyone at the rescue knew about it. Her gaze landed on him, and she knew she was screwed. He'd changed out of his work clothes, wearing jeans and a blue polo shirt that matched his eyes. He'd also took the time to style his dark hair.

That meant he wanted to make an impression.

She wasn't sure how he'd react when he saw Kamden.

Kamden pulled the truck on the side of the Bronco, making sure there was plenty of room on either side. "Someone's early," he grumbled, staring at the stairs where Brett waited.

"Are you going to drop me off?" She wanted to know before she got out of the truck. If she had to face Brett alone, she wanted to be ready. Each time she declined his offers, he smiled and said he'd try again later. His response was sweet at first, but she'd grown annoyed when she learned he meant it.

"I'm not going anywhere until you're settled," Kamden informed her, parking the vehicle and killing the motor. His amber gaze darted over to her. "Unless you want me to go."

"No," she replied quickly, smiling at him. "I want you to stay."

He returned the smile, and it made him look years younger. "Don't try to get out. I'll come around to help you down."

She pulled out her keys, made sure her backpack was zipped and glanced at the side mirror to watch him remove her crutches. For such a large man, he moved quickly and effortlessly. He had to have been athletic in his youth, playing basketball or football. He came to her door, opened it, and reached for her backpack. He slung it over his shoulder and rested the crutches against the door.

"It would be easier if I carried you, but I'm sure you don't want that with company here." He reached out, placing his hands at her waist. "Go slow now."

It wasn't difficult to climb down, not with him keeping her upright, although she was ready to ice her ankle and take the pain medication she'd been given. When she was on her feet, he let her go and handed her the crutches. He stepped aside, watched her get clearance, and closed the door. She approached the stairs but didn't go up them, lifting her head in time to see Brett coming to her.

"Ouch," he said, wincing as he looked at her foot. His eyes traveled up, and their gazes met. His blue eyes were concerned, his expression revealing his worry. "What did the doctor say? How bad is it?"

"Nothing's broken, but the sprain is pretty bad. Brett, this is Kamden." She released the grip on the crutches and motioned between the two men. "Kamden, this is Brett."

The men greeted each other, shook hands, and sized each other up.

"I can stop by with anything you need," Brett offered, eager to establish some sort of footing. He would, of course, as he felt protective of those he cared for. "I can take the dogs to Mindy and come back."

"Thanks, but I'll be fine."

Brett glanced at Kamden. "What if you need help?"

"I won't."

"You shouldn't be alone tonight."

"She's not alone," Kamden entered the conversation, his normal baritone deepening. He inched closer to her and placed a hand against her lower back. "I'll make sure she's taken care of."

Butterflies fluttered in her stomach, and her breath caught. She had a feeling he knew exactly what to do with those hands when he wanted to. He'd been friendly at the cafe but shut down when a group of people had been seated nearby, not wanting anyone to overhear anything he said. For that reason, she thought he'd stand back and let her do all the talking.

"What about tomorrow?" Brett questioned as though he wanted to be sure she had assistance. There was more to it than that, but she wasn't going to say it aloud. "It's a long drive. I'm not that far if she needs something."

"I'm closer," Kamden said, pointing at the house in the distance. "So are my parents."

Brett frowned. "You live with your parents?"

The way Brett said it irked the hell out of her. She responded before Kamden could. "He lives in the white house you saw coming up the mountain. His mom and dad are on the opposite side. They're my neighbors." Wanting to avoid a pissing contest, she cautiously turned toward the trailer. "We need to get the pups reestablished as soon as possible. I fed them this morning, but they'll need to eat in another hour or two."

Brett didn't say anything for several seconds. "I'll drive over to the kennels."

When he went to the Bronco and climbed in, Kamden moved closer. "You weren't kidding, were you?"

"About what?"

"You don't have to chase men."

Brett drove by them, and she hurried to get to her destination. "Brett's harmless."

"Maybe, but he's determined."

The way he said it made her want to grin. "You don't have to be jealous. If I were interested in him, he'd be the one sticking around."

"Is that right?" There was humor in the question. "Any particular reason you're not interested?"

"He spends more time in front of a mirror than me."

His laughter sent a jolt up her spine. "He needs the help. You don't."

Brett opened the back and got to work. There were only four dogs to crate and take to another foster, and it broke her heart seeing him place them in the back of his vehicle. She struggled when they got adopted because she always became attached, but at least she knew they were going to forever homes. This situation felt nothing like that. Mindy was a great foster, and they'd be in good hands, but she wanted to be the one caring for them.

She managed to make it to the back, reaching through the bars to say goodbye to each of them, determined not to cry as the dogs nuzzled her fingers. "Have Mindy call me. I want her to check in and let me know how they are."

"I'll tell her to call as soon as they're settled." Brett softened, recognizing the cause of her distress. When she stepped away, he closed the back, glanced at Kamden, and looked at her. Her stomach knotted, and she hoped he wouldn't say something that caused a fuss. Eventually, he took a deep breath and said, "If you need anything, let me know."

He went on his way, taking Kamden at his word. He climbed into his ride, backed up, and drove away. She stayed where she was as he hit the main road. Her ankle was throbbing, the dull pulsing becoming far more noticeable. She didn't want to bump or move it.

"Drop 'em," Kamden said and inched behind her.

She tried to look over her shoulder to see him. "What?"

He grasped the right crutch, tugged it from her, and tossed it on the ground. Then he slid an arm around her stomach, creating tingles under her skin. "Let the other one go. I've got you."

Who was she to argue? She pulled her arm free and let it fall.

With a shift of his arms, he picked her up. "Where do you want to go?"

She wished she'd moved furniture into the house. She didn't want him anywhere near the trailer. "The house. I want to see Baloo."

"Do you have a bedroom set up?"

Closing her eyes, knowing she was doomed, she shook her head. "Not yet."

"You need to put that foot up and rest." He carried her to the trailer. "I'll get Baloo and bring him to you."

Oh, man. "You're not going to like what you see."

"I've worked on places that belong in hell. I can handle it."

She wasn't sure about that. The trailer had come along with the property since the former tenant no longer wanted it. When she'd brought the U-Haul with her things and taken a look inside, she'd turned around, went to town, and rented a storage unit. Not only was the mobile home small, much of it had been destroyed by years of neglect. She'd blocked off the only bedroom because the floor was caving in. The right amount of weight would cause someone to fall straight through it.

She managed to unlock the door and held her breath when he opened it and brought her inside. Due to diligent work, the place no longer had a musty smell, but there wasn't much room to move around. He stepped into the living area and stopped when he looked at her primary furniture, seeing the couch where she slept.

"Told you," she said, knowing exactly what he saw.

Instead of defending herself, she remained silent.

She couldn't change what she couldn't change.

Kamden's gaze drifted over the living room, went to the kitchen, and stopped when he noticed plywood had been placed in the middle of the hallway. The trailer's exterior looked bad from the passage of time, but he assumed the inside had to be better.

So much for that.

As with the house, the space was clean.

But everything was horrifically crammed.

The crates in the living room would make it impossible

for her to move freely. He recalled thinking she was one of the weirdest women he'd ever met when he found out she lived in the trailer with a pack of dogs, referring to her as the dog lady. Now he was certain her heart was too big for her own good. He wanted to chastise her for putting an animal's comfort above her own. He didn't do so because she'd grown tense in his arms like she'd been admonished for this very thing before.

"Where are your clothes?"

She shifted to peer up at him. "Why?"

"Because you're packing a bag and coming to my place." No way he was letting her stay here. There wasn't enough room, and he worried she'd have difficulty moving around. He didn't want to think about her breaking something else. Before she could disagree, he warned her, "We're not arguing about it. I have a spare bedroom, and there's plenty of space." She narrowed her eyes, not listening to him, so he upped the ante. "It's either that, or I take you to Mom and Dad."

"I'm not leaving Baloo."

If that was the issue, he could remedy it. "We'll bring him with us."

"Are you serious right now?" She hadn't stopped gawking at him, a look of disbelief and shock on her face. "You only started talking to me today. Now you're ready to take me home with you?"

"You wanted us to get to know each other, didn't you?" Maybe if they got up close and personal, she'd decide he wasn't worth the effort. "Don't rile yourself up. If you don't like it at my place, I'll bring you back. But you can't stay here tonight." As he rotated, her feet dinged each other, and she grimaced. "You're already hurting, and you have too much shit to move around to be comfortable. Are your clothes or anything else you need in here? Because I'm about to lock up and take you to the house. We'll get what you need for a couple of days, and you can decide what you want to do."

"This is the craziest day of my life," she muttered, as though she couldn't believe her lot in life. "Everything I need is in the house."

He got out of the shithole as quickly as possible and took her to the house. Before he hit the stairs, he heard Baloo whining. As soon as the door was open and he strode inside, the dog was at his legs, trying to get at the woman in his arms. Deciding it was best, he carried her to the kitchen and took advantage of the chair he'd placed her in earlier. He made sure she was situated before he placed the backpack on the table.

"Where are your things?"

"The laundry room."

He left right away, aware the sun would set soon and the temperature would drop. He went to the laundry room and discovered his task wouldn't be difficult. The dog's food was in a sealed container, and she kept her toiletries in a zippered bag. He put those things together, collected a cardboard box in the corner, and went to the shelf on the far wall to get her clothing. He reached for the overalls she preferred but stopped midway. He chose other items instead, focusing on camisoles, sweaters, and jeans. He tossed several pairs of socks on top of them. When it came to her lacy underwear, he didn't discriminate, snagging panties and bras. His cock reminded him it was there, coming to life as he imagined what she'd look like without clothing.

Fuck.

He never thought he'd bring a woman to his home. In fact, he wouldn't mind if she wanted to bypass the guest bedroom and get comfortable in his bed.

Fuckedy, fuck, fuck.

He gathered her things and made a couple of trips to the truck, making sure to grab the bed the dog had been resting on. He didn't use his extended cab often, but he was grateful for the extra space. He stacked up the things he'd retrieved, leaving a space for Baloo.

Baloo.

The dog's name told him something about the owner— she liked Disney cartoons. He wasn't surprised, but it did remind him of their age difference. He hadn't watched an animated or family-friendly film in over a decade.

Within ten minutes, he had everything moved and ready. He went back to the kitchen, about to step inside, when a soft sound hit his ears. He froze, recognizing the ragged exhales and sniffles. For whatever reason, Everly was upset.

Damn it. This was something he'd never been good at.

A part of him wanted to find something else to do, giving her time to pull herself together, but if he did that, he was nothing but an asshole. Something was bothering her, and he couldn't pretend he didn't notice. With that in mind, he resumed his trek, his gaze landing on her. Baloo had gotten on his back legs, resting his large feet on either side of her, and she'd buried her face into the fur at the dog's neck.

He went over to her and crouched. "What's on your mind, darlin'?"

"It's nothing." She stayed where she was, so he couldn't see her face.

"You want me to be honest with you." He grasped the animal and eased it back, moving the dog aside, wanting her to look at him. "You have to start being honest with me."

Swiping her face against her coat, she said, "The trailer is horrible. It's embarrassing." Her nose was red, and her eyes were slightly puffy when she glanced at him. "There's only so much I can do with the place."

"I know." If he knew anything about her, he knew that. "This isn't the first time I've been in this house. I paid a visit a few years back, right before Frank left. I thought it was about fucking time. He was a good man, but he was one of the filthiest people I've ever met. I thought the floors were beyond repair, but you not only managed to salvage them, you did it on your own. I've seen all the work you've put in. If that's what bothers you, it shouldn't." He noticed the medication on the table. She'd finally broken down and taken something for pain. By now, she had to be exhausted. "You've had a shitty fucking day, and I don't want to make it worse. I have your things ready. If you'll feel more comfortable, I'll take you to Mom and Dad. You know how much they like you, and they'll love having someone to take care of." He rubbed one of Baloo's ears. "They won't mind if you bring furball with you."

"You changed your mind?" She sounded like she'd given up.

The woman was definitely going to kill him.

Or break his goddamned heart.

Fuck it. It was time she understood he wasn't an asshole by pushing her away. He *was* trying to do right by her. Once he got her in his system, he wasn't going to let her go. Since his attempts at explaining didn't seem to be working, it was time to show her just how close she'd gotten to the fire.

He didn't warn her, crowding her space.

He slid his fingers into the loose hair at her nape, getting a firm grip, and lifted himself. Their gazes met, and her hazel eyes darkened, her pupils dilating. A little voice in his head told him that he couldn't take it back once he did this, but he didn't give a shit. It had been years since he'd thought about a woman like this. He'd told her how he would be if she wanted to be with him, and he'd given her fair warning.

He pulled her to him, intentionally being rough, and brought her mouth to his. He didn't wait for permission, bringing his tongue out and flicking it against her lower lip. When she gasped and her mouth opened, he delved into the wet cavern, deepening the kiss, reveling in the first taste of her. He held her in a way that made it impossible for her to break free, keeping her head where he wanted it. She tried to shift her torso, and he brought his free hand to her hip, pinning her in place with his palm and fingers. She moaned, letting him take control, and he hummed in approval. Making the kiss more aggressive, he clutched the delicate bones of her pelvis in such a way that she'd feel the imprint of his hand long after the kiss ended.

His sex-deprived body responded to her nearness, his cock hardening like a baseball bat. His balls pulsed as his heart rate increased. If she'd been feeling better, he'd have plucked her from the chair and taken her to the counter. Once there, he'd have unbuttoned the overalls, tugged them down, and planted a hand between her legs. He'd make sure to tease her through her panties, wanting to know how hot and wet she was. He wouldn't hook his fingers around the thin garment and move it aside until she was begging him to touch her.

His thoughts got dirtier, his need palpable.

He released her hip, letting her squirm, and firmly cupped her pussy. She inhaled raggedly, arching her back, pressing against his palm. He rubbed his thumb over the material shielding her clit, applying a steady amount of pressure. She grasped his arm, her nails digging into his coat. He considered taking her all the way, upping the ante until she climaxed, but he wanted that to happen in his bed. After he removed her clothes and touched her all over, he'd give her what she wanted.

He removed the hand between her legs, getting a handle on himself. She fought for air, panting softly. There might be differences between them, but their chemistry was undeniable. He reined in his desire, forcing it back, and used the hand in her hair to pull her away. Her eyes were dazed, her lips slightly swollen.

"So what'll it be?" His voice thickened and lowered several octaves. "My place or theirs?"

"Yours." She exhaled the word.

With the beauty of her response, he wasn't sure he could keep his hands or mouth to himself. "I'm done playing nice. You want me? The feeling is absolutely fucking mutual. I've told you how I am, but you're right. There is more to it. I'm not always polite or easygoing. I'm not sure what it was like with your former lovers, but I'll be hard, demanding, and I'll wear your pretty little ass out." He lowered his hand, resting it on the curve of her buttock. A tremor shot through her, and he gave her rear a squeeze. "I want to make sure that this is what you want. Take a minute and think about it. You need to be sure, Everly."

She didn't hesitate or think about shit. "I'm sure."

If that's how she wanted to play, he was game. He came to her this time, pressing a chaste kiss to her mouth, and slid his fingers from her hair. As he rose, he watched her, wanting to see how she'd react to the sizeable tent in his jeans. Her gazes hovered over the area, but she didn't seem offended or shocked. Seeing that, aware she picked up what he'd put down, he placed the medication in her backpack, zipped it up, and lifted it from the table.

"I'm going to put Baloo in the truck. I'll be right back."

He patted his leg and got the dog's attention. Baloo seemed happy about that, trotting on over. He patted the animal's broad head before he guided it from the room. He reached down to adjust himself before he stepped outside, knowing he'd be aroused until he took things to another level. The woman was amazing, taking what he had to give, squirming around like she couldn't wait for more. If this was any indication of things, they'd burn each other alive. Opening the back door and encouraging the dog to jump into the rear passenger seat, he lifted his head.

His mother and father had been shoving Everly down his throat for weeks, telling him how amazing she was, encouraging him to visit and help her out. That was part of the reason he'd avoided her so diligently. After what had just happened in the kitchen, he thought his parents were on to something.

He wanted to ravish her silly and pamper her afterward. He imagined what it would be like if they got into a routine, knowing just what the other wanted and needed. It had been so long—*too fucking long*—since he'd been like this. For the very first time, he didn't give a shit about Delaney or his past.

He was flying blind without a parachute.

And he was excited as hell.

CHAPTER FIVE

EVERLY HAD SEEN Kamden's home each time she ventured to town. She loved the wraparound porch, finding it lovely. But she hadn't realized how impressive the house truly was until he carried her inside and flipped a switch to turn on the LED ceiling lights. He hadn't been kidding when he said there was plenty of space to move around. He'd chosen real oak for the hardwood floors and had gone for an open interior layout. There weren't many decorations, his furnishings large, dark, and simple. The living room was to the right, and his enormous kitchen was directly in front of them. She noted two hallways branched out on both sides.

He carried her to a large leather recliner near the door and eased her down. When her ass hit the cushioned leather, he helped her pull off her coat and let her go. He put the large jacket on a hanger by the door and snagged the satellite controller on the end table. His gaze drifted to her as he handed the remote over.

"Take a breather. I'll get Baloo."

As he left, she reclined in the comfortable chair and closed her eyes. She thought about the kiss he'd given her. The first lap of his tongue had curled her toes. Shortly after that, a fire built in her belly. If not for her clothing, he'd have seen her nipples harden. She could still feel his hand against her mound, squirming when she imagined his thumb stroking her clit. He knew exactly what he was doing, using just enough pressure. One touch from him soaked her panties. She'd thought he was gentle but quickly learned he could be rough too.

That intrigued her, making her want him even more.

Good lord, the man went to her head like whiskey.

She heard the click of Baloo's nails and turned her head, seeing Kamden right behind him. He'd brought the canine's enormous dog bed into the house. He strode over and plopped it down beside her. The dog marched over and took a seat, resting his head on the arm of the recliner.

"He's well behaved," he said, stroking Baloo's head.

That made her smile. She knew how good her boy was, but it hadn't always been easy. "You should have met him when he was a puppy. He chewed everything in sight."

"Will he let me know if he needs to go out?"

Nodding, she answered, "He'll go to the door and bark."

"Are you hungry? I have chili in the Crock-Pot."

She wasn't all that hungry. Not for food, anyway. "I'm good."

"What about big boy here?" Her heart melted when she saw Baloo's face. He'd closed his eyes, leaning into Kamden's hand. "I'm assuming he needs to eat."

"He gets two scoops. There's a measuring cup in the container. The lid can be flipped around and used as a bowl if he needs one."

"I can wrestle up a couple of dishes. Let me get your things first."

He turned to leave, and she watched him, getting a good look at his ass. She didn't think she'd ever seen a man that literally looked good enough to eat. He left the door open as he went outside. It took two trips to bring everything into the house. He closed the door, placed a cardboard box and her backpack behind the recliner, and carried the dog food container into the kitchen. He vanished around the corner, and she wondered just how big the house was. She heard a cabinet open, followed by dishes clinking together. The distinct sound of kibble being poured into a bowl echoed through the open space. She didn't have to tell Baloo it was time to eat. He shot off, running toward the sound.

Her eyes slid closed again, and she tried to fight the grips of sleep. The medication had helped with the pain, but it made her groggy as hell. She realized she'd drifted off when a spring beneath her vibrated. Kamden lifted the footrest, taking care as he shifted her legs up. He had an ice pack in his hand.

"Oops, sorry," she murmured, swiping at her face.

"Don't apologize. You're here to rest and relax."

"Is that all?" A part of her couldn't believe she'd said it aloud.

He removed her boot that kept her ankle stable, cocking a brow. "Don't tempt me."

After the kiss he'd given her, how could she not? Sex was all she could think about. Judging by the way he'd gone about things, she knew he wouldn't be anything like her prior boyfriends. They didn't do much foreplay and lived for quickies. She'd always wondered what it would be like to have an aggressive partner who wanted more than a five-minute marathon that often left her sexually frustrated.

He put the ice on her ankle. "There you go. You need anything?"

Was he serious? Couldn't he tell how aroused she was?

His wicked grin told her he knew what was on her mind. "You're a naughty little thing, aren't you?" Her cheeks heated as embarrassment slammed into her. She'd never been this bold or brazen. He crouched beside her, placing a hand on her knee. "Tonight, you're going to rest." He must have known she wasn't happy about it because he chuckled. "Don't worry, I'll make it up to you. I'll put a smile on your face tomorrow."

Ugh. Tomorrow. "Don't you have to work?"

He removed his coat, hung it up, and pulled his phone from his back pocket. "I'm going to take care of that. I also need to call my brother. He left a message, so whatever he needs must be important."

"You mean the mysterious Brady your mom talks about?"

"Don't get any ideas." His gaze darted to her, a hidden warning within his eyes. He'd told her he was possessive, and she was looking right at it. "He's taken."

She couldn't help herself, pushing him again. "What about you?"

"When I said you are going to rest, I meant it. If you don't watch yourself," he warned, prowling over to her, "I'm going to yank you out of that chair and bust your ass."

"You wouldn't dare."

He snagged one of her braids, wrapped it around his hand, and lowered his head until they were eye level. His eyes had darkened, the lust in his expression shutting her up. He leaned closer, leaving a few inches between them.

"Not only do I mean it, I'll get you so turned on you'll be squirming in my lap and begging to come, but I won't let you. I'll work you up, get you soaked, and make you go to bed needy and wet." He made sure they were staring right at each other, giving her hair a tug. "You going to be good? Or do you want to see if I'm as good as my word?"

Sweet baby J. "You'd do that to me?"

"Only one way to find out."

No way she was risking it. "I'll be good."

"That's my girl." He gave her a chaste kiss, released her hair, and stepped back. "I'm going to call Bray, then I'll take care of work. I suggest you close those eyes and let the ice and medicine work."

Or else he'll work me up and leave me needy and wet.

Damn.

She did as he said, leaning back and closing her eyes. Even when he stroked her head, she didn't move, open her mouth, or look at him. He was too tempting, and she didn't want to see if he meant what he said.

If he cranked things up another notch, she'd lose her mind.

Kamden went to his bedroom, deciding then and there she'd be sleeping in his bed. He wasn't going to take things further since the pain medication had doped her up. He wanted her head clear when he took her. If she did as he asked—getting the rest she needed—he'd reward her in a way that wouldn't involve her moving at all.

She obviously wanted relief, so it wouldn't take much.

He dialed his brother as he took clean linens from the closet. When the line clicked over, Brady's voice came through the line. "It's about time. I was wondering if you were ever going to call back."

"I'm a busy man. What can I say?"

"Busy, my ass," Brady grumbled. "Try doing my job."

No way. One officer in the family was enough.

A shooting not so long ago had put his parents in a state of panic for weeks. They supported Brady, but they didn't like what he did for a living.

"Thanks for the offer, but I'll have to pass. You want to tell me what's up?"

"I'm calling because I need your help with something."

That was unusual. His younger brother usually tackled things on his own. Since Brady had recently gotten involved with a woman named Candice, Kamden worried something had happened. He put the bedding down and sat on the edge of the bed.

"What's wrong?"

"Nothing's wrong. I wanted to see if you can make a

trip to see me this week."

"I thought you were coming here next weekend." His brother had told him he was going on a trip with his lady and would be stopping by on his way to Florida.

Brady drew a deep breath like he was preparing himself for something. "I am, but I want to have a ring before we leave. I need help picking one out."

Holy shit. "You're proposing?"

"Sure am."

The pair had only been together a couple of months. "That was fast."

"When you find the one for you, it's what you do." Brady chuckled, and Kamden could picture his grin through the phone. "You wanted me to get Mom and Dad off your ass. I thought you'd thank me."

Damn. He had told Brady the sooner he got married and had some babies, the better. Their parents wanted grandchildren in the worst way. Back then, he'd planned on staying away from Everly. He had no clue he'd be bringing her home with him.

"When do you need me there?" The drive took a few hours, but he could make a round trip in a day.

"I was hoping tomorrow afternoon. Candice has to go to her office. It'll give me time to slip out before she notices. I want to go to Devida's. I've heard they're the best."

Devida's.

Kamden hadn't been there since he'd bought Delaney's engagement ring over a decade ago. After their breakup, she'd kept the expensive piece of jewelry. Not that he wanted the fucking thing back. There were too many bad memories. If she'd offered it to him, he probably would have thrown it in the trash.

"If you can't find what you want there, you probably won't find it anywhere," he said. "They have just about everything."

"So you'll come?"

Damn it. Brady never asked for much, so Kamden couldn't say no. But he didn't want to leave Everly on her own. "I can come, but I won't be alone. I'll have to bring someone with me."

"Who might that be?"

He lowered his voice, not wanting Everly to overhear. He'd referred to her in one way when he'd spoken to Brady about her, giving her a nickname that wasn't very nice. "The dog girl."

"Are you fucking with me? The dog girl?" Brady's tone went from blissful to serious. "I thought you were avoiding her."

It was time to come clean. "Not anymore."

Brady didn't speak for several seconds. His brother knew all about Delaney. He'd been there to help Kamden pick up the pieces. They'd had a conversation about broken hearts when Brady confessed he had a woman in his life. Kamden had told his sibling to love the hell out of Candice, and apparently, his brother planned on doing just that.

"Are you happy?" Brady asked like he was afraid to.

"I'm not sure yet," he answered honestly. "She's something else. That's for sure."

"If you can't get away, I can shop on my own."

Typical Brady, always doing the right thing. "It's fine, Bray. I'm glad you called. I have to call in to work anyway. What time do you want me there?"

"Two o'clock would be great. If you're bringing the dog—" Brady stopped immediately, ever the gentleman who put women on a pedestal. "I'm not calling her that. What's her actual name?"

Glancing at the door, lowering his voice again, he whispered, "Everly."

"Oh man, Kam." Brady groaned. "You're talking like that for a reason. She's at your place right now, isn't she?"

"It's not what you think." Brady knew he preferred to sex women up and walk away immediately after. For that reason, he explained himself. "I went to help her today. She took a tumble and sprained her ankle. I had to take her to the emergency clinic. She needs help the next couple of days."

"Have you told Mom and Dad?"

Fuck. Brady knew their parents liked her. With that kernel of knowledge, his sibling knew they'd have Kamden's head if he hurt her. "We just made it home. You're the first person I've talked to."

"If she's coming with you, it means you like her."

You don't say. "Obviously, idiot."

"I wasn't trying to be an ass." Brady cleared his throat, making it evident he wasn't sure what to say. "If you want, we could make a night of it. I'll tell Candice you wanted to take a break and visit, and we can go out to eat. It'll give us a chance to catch up. Our girls can get to know each other."

That wasn't a bad idea, but he didn't want to keep Everly in a truck all day and night. "We'll need a place to stay overnight."

"That's not a problem. Candice is busy packing for the trip, so we're staying at her apartment for the next couple of days. You're free to use my place."

"Are you sure?" Kamden questioned, reminded there was another obstacle if he drove to Tennessee. It was his brother's home, so he had to be honest. "She'll want to bring Baloo."

"Who the hell is Baloo?"

"Her dog."

"You mean the one that's as big as a pony?" Brady asked.

That's exactly how he described the beast. "That's the one."

"He's not going to destroy my house is he?"

"Believe it or not, he's the best-mannered dog I've ever come across. He doesn't jump on you and listens to commands. She obviously spent a lot of time training him."

"Glad to hear it. Hold on a minute," Brady said, and Kamden heard him shuffling the phone. Candice's voice carried in the background, asking if Brady wanted to watch a movie. He told her he'd join her in a minute and came back to the phone. "Sorry about that."

"Movie night?"

"Could be, if it's a good one. If not, we'll find other ways to entertain ourselves."

Kamden knew what that meant. "I bet you will."

"Should I expect you tomorrow?"

"I'll leave in the morning and stop by your place. Call me when you want to meet."

"Thanks, Kam."

"Not a problem."

He heard Candice calling for Brady in the background. "I've got to go. Duty calls."

"Better take care of it. Talk to you soon."

As soon as the call ended, he contacted another property manager, asking him to swing by his current project and make sure things were in order for the next couple of days. Since they often covered for each other, it wasn't an issue. He hung up and reached out to Chris, letting his friend know he'd be out of town. With that done, he put the phone on the dresser, stripped the bed and replaced the linens, and put the dirty bedding in the laundry basket.

He returned to the living room, discovering Everly had fallen asleep. Baloo rested on the bed beside her, keeping a close watch. He hadn't asked her about the dog, but it was apparent she adored the creature and it loved her. If her father died not too long ago, the animal was probably the only companionship she had.

No wonder she was so lonely.

He went to the couch, collected the throw blanket his mother had given him several Christmases ago and went to cover her. As soon as it touched her, her lashes fluttered, and she blinked several times.

"It's all right," he whispered, wanting to get something to eat before he carried her to bed. "Go back to sleep."

She groaned, shifting her body. "Where are the crutches?"

He'd left them where he'd stored them. "In the back of the truck."

"Can you get them for me?"

"What do you need? I'll bring it to you."

She sighed, peering up at him. "You can bring me the toilet?"

She really is a little smart-ass. "No, but I can take you to it."

Her face reddened, and she narrowed her eyes. "You're not watching me use the bathroom."

He lifted the blanket from her. "Didn't say I was."

"Hold up." She lifted a hand, gazing at him. "Where did you put my clothes?"

He tossed the plush throw on the couch and brought her the cardboard box. She sorted through it and frowned. "You didn't get my jammies?"

"I didn't see any." Everything had been neatly lined up. He wouldn't have missed them.

She scowled and rolled her eyes. "They were in the dryer."

He removed the ice pack and placed it on the coffee table. "I'm not a mind reader, darlin'."

"I'm not blaming you," she sighed and selected a camisole, purple yoga pants, and a thick pair of socks. She also collected the bag with her toiletries. "I didn't think about it."

"You want a shower?" Simply thinking about her under steamy water got him hard. "I can drop you off and pick you up when you're done."

"Drop me off and pick me up?" Her laughter was addictive, sultry, and sweet. She shot him an impish grin, and he wanted to snatch her up and kiss the hell out of her. "Like school?"

"Just like school," he replied, picking her up, "only better."

He took her to his private bathroom since it had everything she needed. Baloo trotted behind him, and he wondered if the dog followed her everywhere. He stepped inside and sat her on the edge of the bathtub. He didn't offer to run her a bath, worried she could slip and fall climbing in and out of it. While he could offer to take one with her, he meant what he said earlier. Tonight he wanted her to rest and unwind.

"I know you built this place, but did you design it, too?"

"Pretty much." He opened a cabinet, got a towel, and placed it near the sink. Then he went to the walk-in shower and got the water running. Gazing over his shoulder, he asked, "You like it?"

"It's beautiful."

He glanced around, looking at the things he'd installed himself. He'd been picky since it was where he wanted to live the rest of his life. "I'm glad you think so."

"I can take it from here." She placed her garments on the counter beside her, pulling the rubber bands from her hair.

He was sure she could, but he wanted her to know he wasn't far away. "I'm leaving the door open." When she acted like she might argue, he explained, "If you need something, I'll hear you. I won't come in unless you tell me to." Since he was making himself food, he wanted to see if she'd changed her mind about dinner. "I'm going to grab some chili. You want some?"

She started unbraiding her hair. "I'm good."

"By the way," he said slowly, curious how she'd react, thinking it was better to tell her now instead of in the morning, "we're taking a trip tomorrow."

Running her fingers through the slightly tangled strands, she titled her head and looked at him. "We are?"

"My brother needs me to help him with something. He wants us to go out with him and his girl after. He said we can stay at his place. That all right with you?"

Her fingers stilled. "Are you sure you want me to go?"

He didn't like the way she looked at him, like she thought he was going to hide her in a closet and pretend she didn't exist. True, he'd been a prick, but he was starting to turn a corner. After she met his brother, he hoped she'd understand that when he did something, he didn't do it half-assed.

"I wouldn't ask otherwise," he informed her.

"What about Baloo?"

So his gut instinct had been right. She wouldn't go without the dog. "He's coming too."

"When do we leave?"

No fuss, no muss. It worked for him. "In the morning. It'll take a few hours to make it there. If we leave early enough, we can have lunch as soon as we arrive."

"All right."

He didn't want to leave, itching to see her disrobe, but he exited the room.

There would be plenty of time to discover every inch of her body. She might not know it, but he'd been serious when he'd told her he was going to put a smile on her face tomorrow. If he had his way, they'd both be sporting grins as they made the trip.

He was going to eat her up.

CHAPTER SIX

After her shower, Everly had gotten changed. It had been a struggle to hop on one leg, but she managed to get dressed and brush her teeth. She hadn't called for Kamden, aware he'd taken a seat to eat, so she'd made it to the bed and plopped down. Her eyes had been heavy and she'd drifted off. Kamden had tucked her in and told her to go back to sleep at some point. His bed had been so comfortable, she'd crashed immediately. She thought she remembered him curving his large body around her, holding her tight as she dozed, but the memory was fuzzy.

She groaned as she came to awareness, wondering how long she'd been out, and noticed a hint of light coming from the window. Since she could smell coffee, and Kamden wasn't with her, it had to be early in the morning. Taking care, making sure her foot was clear of the blankets, she eased from the bed and went into the bathroom. She went about her normal routine, combing out her hair, splashing cold water on her face, and brushing her teeth.

As she patted her skin dry, her eyes drifted to the mirror.

She jumped when she saw Kamden standing in the doorway.

"We're going to have to work on our communication," he said, humor in his tone, his eyes that beautiful shade of gold she could drown in. "I told you if you needed anything to call for me."

He stepped into the bathroom, and she placed the washcloth on the sink. Aside from an unbuttoned pair of jeans, he didn't have on a stitch of clothing. She took him in, her gaze roaming over the contours of his chest, discovering he was muscular and lean with a visible six-pack. He didn't have hair on his chest, which only brought attention to the treasure trail that started below his belly button, traveled down, and disappeared behind denim. She took him in, wondering if she'd bitten off more than she could chew.

He was all man. Not at all like the boys she'd dated.

He didn't stop, silent as a cat, coming behind her. His arm slid around her waist, and he pressed himself against her back, making sure she felt the sizable erection prodding her ass. Despite the clothing between them, she could feel how long and thick he was.

"Good morning, sunshine. Do you remember what I said last night?" He nuzzled her neck, rubbing his bristled chin against her shoulder. "It's tomorrow."

His words came back to her, making her pussy clench. *I'll put a smile on your face tomorrow.*

She almost sank into a puddle at his feet when he confirmed what she suspected. She'd fanaticized about him. Even hours ago, she thought about what he'd be like, getting annoyed when he told her to rest and stop testing him. Now that she was facing the real deal, she felt awkward and shy. She wasn't all that experienced. He'd figure that out right away. What if he didn't like that? What if she couldn't please him in the way he expected her to?

His lips drifted to her ear. "Is that a no?"

She answered by moving, rotating her hips, creating friction against his cock. His hand drifted up, cupped her chin, and forced her to look in the mirror. Their eyes met in the reflection, their expressions revealing they both wanted what was about to happen. The arm around her waist loosened, and she trembled as his fingers drifted over her side and flatted his hand over her stomach.

"If you want this, you need to tell me."

She felt tongue-tied but managed to speak. "I want this."

He released her and stepped back. Grasping the hem of her camisole, he pulled the thin covering over her head. She wasn't busty and hadn't worn a bra, so her breasts were revealed immediately. He tossed the garment aside and returned, cupping the mounds, giving them a squeeze. Heat burst in her belly and rushed to her nipples and sex. Her legs felt wobbly, forcing her to put her hands on the counter for balance.

"Very nice," he rasped, giving her ear a nip. "Now for the rest."

He skimmed his fingers down, bringing them to her pants. He slipped them beneath the stretchy material as he got a grip and tugged them from her hips. She lowered her head, lifting her feet when he took them off. When he returned, she only had on a lacy pair of underwear.

"Fuck, baby. Look at you." He groaned, running his hand over her ass. "When God put you together, He knew exactly what He was doing."

Her breath caught when he wrapped his arms around her and lifted her off her feet. He spun them around, taking her into the bedroom. He made sure her feet hit the ground before he turned her, cautious as she could only bear weight on one leg. She rested her hands on his biceps, feeling the muscles flex. His fingers tickled her back as he brought his hand up and fisted her hair. He applied pressure, forcing her to lift her chin.

When she peered up at him, he studied her. "I've never lied to a woman, and I'm not starting now. I told you how I am. You know how it'll be with me. Once I have you, I'm not likely to let go. Are you sure about this? "

Abso-fucking-lutely. "I'm sure."

Unlike his previous kiss, this one was teasing, his tongue darting against hers and pulling away. She followed his lead, doing the same thing, clinging to him like a kitten. She could taste coffee, sugar, and a hint of Irish cream. She moaned when he cupped her ass, giving it a hard squeeze, and inched closer to her. Their chests touched, her nipples brushing against his skin. When he urged her back, guiding her to the bed, she sank to the mattress.

"Lay back." His voice had changed, becoming deep and authoritative.

She carefully lowered herself, and he hooked his fingers into her underwear. As he tugged them from her hips and slipped them off, he nudged her knees apart. She was grateful she kept things tidy down below, trembling as he pressed a kiss to her thigh.

"Spread your legs and make room. I've been thinking about going down on you since last night."

Oh dear God.

Fisting the bedding beneath her and taking a breath for courage, she slowly parted them and gazed at the ceiling. If he noticed her nerves, he didn't let on. "Damn, darlin'. Your pussy is so soft and pink. I'm going to enjoy this just as much as you."

She gasped when he parted her labia with his thumbs, finding the courage to gaze down at him. His eyes darted up, and her heart skipped a beat, her blood pounding in her ears. Not only was he going to go down on her, the man looked like he was about to devour her whole. He placed her legs over his shoulders and didn't sever eye contact, bringing his tongue out, giving her a long, hard lick. He followed that up with another. Then another. Her eyes crossed, making it impossible to see, and she tossed her head back.

He took his time, lapping at her labia, flicking his tongue up and down her slit. The man knew what he was doing without question, making her ridiculously wet, paving the way for the finger he eased into her. He pumped his hand, keeping a steady pace. He used the same technique, moving his tongue harder and faster, getting into a dizzying rhythm. She couldn't stop shaking, feeling the delicious warmth in her belly that told her she was close. Her hips moved on their own, following the path that would give her relief.

"Oh, God, Kamden," she moaned.

He pulled away to ask, "Do you want to come?"

"Yes."

He gave a low growl, adding another finger to the first as he lapped at her. He stretched her vaginal walls, rotated his wrist, and rubbed. He stopped when he hit her sweet spot, and she cried out. He paid close attention to the sensitive area, stroking it over and over.

She whimpered, thrusting her pussy against his face and hand, struggling as she tried to breathe. He drew her clit into his mouth. The heat pulsing through her overflowed, and it felt like her entire body shattered. It had been so long she didn't try to be quiet, crying out as she came. She dug her nails into the comforter, flying so high she never wanted to come down. He didn't stop, suckling the bundle of nerves, plunging his fingers in and out of her.

The bliss and relief made everything feel better, leaving her completely content and relaxed. She took deep breaths, aware her heart was pounding. The fingers inside her vanished, and she felt Kamden kissing her thighs again. The bed shifted as he stood, and she knew he could see the shit-eating grin on her face.

The distinct sound of a zipper being lowered had her opening her eyes and sitting up. He had a condom in his hand, the wrapper already ripped open.

He handed it over and instructed, "Get me ready for you."

She wasn't sure what he meant, so she placed the rubber on the bed, clutched the top of his jeans, and pulled them down. His cock sprang free, larger and thicker than she'd ever seen. The meaty head was seeping, a bead of pre-come oozing from the slit in the tip. She wrapped her hand around the base, and he responded by sliding his fingers into her hair.

"Suck me." He gave the strands a tug. "Take me deep."

In a smooth motion, she drew him into her mouth. His salty taste burst on her tongue, and she moaned, sucking him down. He was too broad and long to take completely, so she used her hand, bobbing her head, taking as much as possible.

"Damn, you are a sight. I love seeing your lips stretched around my cock." Kamden voiced his approval, bucking his hips. "I knew your mouth would feel good." His motions got harsher and he touched the back of her throat. "Keep going, baby."

She tried, sucking on him like a sweet treat, increasing her grip on the base as she worked his length with her hand. He groaned, moving faster, and she tasted more of him on her tongue.

"Next time, I'm going to come in your mouth. I'm going to watch you swallow me down." He pulled her away, angling her head to meet his eyes. His irises had changed color again, becoming dark brown. "This time, I want to be inside you. I want to see your face when you take every inch of me."

Her heart was pounding, her sex clenching.

She'd thought about this for weeks, ever since she first laid eyes on him. She'd thought it was a pipe dream, something that would remain out of her reach. She picked up the wrapper and pulled the condom free.

She couldn't believe this was happening.

Kamden tried to put a leash on his lust. If they didn't have to leave soon, he'd have come down her throat, took a breather, and went at her again. She tasted as good as she smelled, spicy and sweet. He thought she was hiding a nice body beneath her clothing, but his wildest imaginings didn't come close. She was lean but curvy where it counted, her body in perfect proportion with her frame. With her glorious mane cascading around her shoulders, the wavy locks vibrant and soft, she looked like something out of a fucking dream.

When she rolled the condom on, taking more time than necessary, he knew his assumptions were correct. The way she cried out when she came, the sound echoing off the walls, meant she hadn't had sex in a long time.

But it was more than that.

She'd been nervous when he went down on her, acting like it was something she wasn't used to. She'd said she had two boyfriends, and neither of the assholes had taken the time to appreciate her sexually. He was about to take care of that, showing her everything and more. If she'd let him, he'd keep her in the bed a majority of the time.

He grasped her waist, helping her slide back, and lowered his body over hers. As he fingered her, her wet and snug cunt had clamped down on his fingers. He was almost certain her pussy would strangle his cock. He took her in, pissed at himself for pushing her away for so long. Fuck, she was beautiful with her long hair spread all over the bed and her lips pink and swollen. Her eyes were always expressive, revealing her emotions. Right now, she was primed, eager, and ready for him. Moving between her legs, he fisted himself. He coated the tip with the wetness between her legs and lodged the head against her. She wrapped her hands around his back and sank her nails into his skin.

Little hellcat.

He took his time, sliding into her slowly, watching her

face just like he told her he would. As rough as he could be, now wasn't the time. He had to be cautious and get her used to him. Her eyes shuttered, her lips parting. She was just as tight as he thought she'd be, hugging him like a second skin. He had to ask her about birth control. Eventually, he wanted to feel her without the condom. He was halfway in when she gazed up at him, eyes growing wide with panic.

"Easy." He pulled back slightly, thrust into her gently, and used the lubrication from her body to clear the way. "Let me take care of it. I won't hurt you."

"Oh my." She exhaled the words, arching her back. "Oh, God."

"Almost there. Relax." He waited until she did and kept going, grinding his teeth. He exhaled roughly when he sank the rest of the way into her, his testicles hitting her ass, and closed his eyes. He didn't move, awash in sensation. "Fuck, you're tight."

It shouldn't be possible for anyone to as feel as good as she did. A part of him didn't want to move, staying inside her as long as she'd let him. The tingle in his spine meant he wouldn't last long. He actually regretted that, wanting to take more time with her.

"That feels...it's so..." She flexed her vaginal muscles.

He groaned. "It's so what?"

Licking her lips, she answered, "Different."

"How does it feel different, baby?"

She hesitated like she was afraid to tell him. "I feel you all over. Inside and out."

"Do you like it?" He didn't have to ask, hearing it in her voice, but he wanted to make sure. He rocked against her carefully. "Does it feel good?"

She moved her hands to his lower back. "Mm-hmm."

"That's what I want to hear."

Clenching his teeth, he retreated from the fisting haven, stopping when only the head was inside her. He returned

72

quickly, spearing into her. He repeated himself, finding a steady motion, bringing a hand to her ass to guide her. Dipping his head, he lavished attention on her nipples, licking and sucking, alternating between them. He gave her a couple of nips, seeing how she'd react, and grinned when her hands left his back and slid into his hair. He kept going, repeating the actions until he felt her pussy clenching him.

"You feel amazing." He lifted his head, bringing his mouth to hers. "So tight and hot. I could stay inside you forever."

He kissed her again, feeling his balls going taut, and increased the pace, becoming rougher. Wanting her to come with him, he snaked his hand between them, found her clit, and rubbed his fingers against her. She tensed beneath him, holding him closer. He snapped his hips, using more force. Her breathing turned erratic, her movements no longer fluid or smooth.

He brought his lips to her ear and whispered. "Let go, Everly. I've got you."

In five thrusts, her eyes slammed shut, and he felt her cunt rippling around him. Her pussy milked him, bringing him over with her. He groaned and lifted her slightly, sinking as far as he could into her. He held her there, basking in the moment, feeling like the weight of the fucking world wasn't on his shoulders. He stayed where he was for several seconds, taking in what they'd done, knowing he'd offered her something he didn't think he would. She'd given him a chance, and he sure as hell was going to do the same. He made sure to bring his elbows up, not wanting to rest all of his weight on her as he eased down and came back to reality.

She placed her forehead on his shoulder. "That was incredible."

"Wait until that ankle of yours heals." Once she could move, he'd take her in ways that would blow her mind.

"I'll show you incredible."

She gave a hum of approval. "I'd like that."

"I know you will. I'll make sure of it."

He didn't want to leave her, but they needed to get ready. They had to be on the road in an hour. He eased out of her, holding the condom in place. As soon as he rose, he removed it, tied it off, and threw it into the small trash can beside the bed. With that out of the way, he returned to her, taking her hand.

"Come on, sweetness," he said, helping her to her feet. "Let's get you clean."

He kept her upright as he took her into the bathroom, opened the glass door, and turned on the shower. He managed to lean over and retrieve two towels. When he placed them on the counter and turned, he saw her trying to cover herself. Poor thing. This was all new to her. She'd get over that embarrassment soon enough. Before long, she wouldn't even think about clothing when she was around him. To take her mind off that, he tested the water, found it heated and ready, and grabbed a washcloth. As he assisted her inside, he brought her to the spray and put her hands on the wall.

"Stay there."

He went to work, soaping up the cloth, brushing the plush material over her back, ass, and legs. When satisfied, he snaked an arm around her and took care of her stomach, neck, and paid careful attention when he washed the area between her legs. His gaze drifted down, and he got another look at her ankle. He winced, seeing how swollen and bruised it was. He'd make sure to bring ice packs along. If he pushed the seat in the truck back, he could elevate it somewhat. One thing was certain, she needed to get the hell off it.

"Do you want your own shampoo?" He leaned forward, rested his chin on her shoulder, and brushed his lips against her cheek.

Her head lifted, and her multicolored eyes met his. "You're going to wash my hair?"

"You're getting full-service, darlin'."

"Conditioner too?" It wasn't a question but a challenge.

Sassy thing. "If that's what you want."

Her mischievous smile tugged at his heart. "They're on the counter."

He got them and returned, getting down to business. It turned out to be more difficult than he expected, her hair so long and thick he spent minutes washing it. She showed him how to apply the conditioner, giggling when he stroked her side and tickled her, revealing how happy and giddy she could be. The interaction made him feel young again, taking him back to who he used to be, allowing his carefree nature to come out from hiding.

When he was done, he had a simple request. "Will you wear it loose for me?"

She rolled her eyes, still playful. "What is it with men and hair?"

"Haven't you heard?" He teased her, running a finger down her spine. "Cavemen like to drag their women around with it."

"I thought about chopping it off. I even made an appointment."

Hell no. "Don't you dare." He put his palm on the top of her head and stroked the length of it, finding the conditioner gave it a silky texture. He stopped when he came to the middle of her back. "It suits you, and I love the way it feels against my skin." Wrapping his arms around her, getting as close as possible, he asked, "Will you wear it down?"

"When do we have to leave?"

"In the next thirty minutes or so, if you want me to buy you lunch."

"I need to get dressed and dry it."

That worked for him. He needed to take the dog out

and put their things in the truck. He cleaned himself quickly, shut off the water, and opened the glass door. He got a towel, eager to dry her off. She reached to take it from him, and he tsked her, patting her skin softly. He took his time, looking her over, letting his hands linger. He'd actually missed this part of things. Sex was well and good, but he enjoyed pampering a woman. It had been so long since he'd done it. He'd forgotten how good it felt.

When he finished, he handed her the towel. "I'll get your clothes and put them on the bed. If you need anything, give me a yell. I don't want you moving around if you don't have to."

As she stared at him, a rosy flush on her cheeks, he saw her as the young woman she was. She'd never been completely loved by a man—that was obvious—but she wanted to be. He decided to be greedy, moving in for another kiss. She was right there with him, opening her mouth, giving as good as she got. They licked, nibbled, and slid their tongues together. He couldn't wait until she was completely mended. He wanted to take her on the counter, the floor, the wall, and anywhere else that tickled his fancy.

Thinking about the sounds she made had his cock rising again.

Aware he'd keep her naked if he didn't leave, he snatched his towel and dried himself as he went to the bedroom. He planned on talking to her as they drove, getting to know more about her, letting her know what he'd like to happen between them. He'd thought he wouldn't be able to let her go once he got her in his system, and he'd been right. They'd have to figure out how things would work, but he wasn't letting her live in that fucking trailer. She could stay with him, and he'd take her to work on the house if she asked him to. Hell, he'd finish the bastard thing if it meant he could spend more time with her.

As he dressed, he came to an important realization, going still as it was something he'd never expected. He felt light on his feet and content, excited to greet the day. He wanted to make her smile and laugh.

She might not know it, but she'd changed everything.

For him and for her.

The captivating creature had him wrapped him around her little finger.

CHAPTER SEVEN

EVERLY TOOK IN the house Kamden had brought her to, studying the porch. A few flower pots were hanging from the top railing. The plants weren't in bloom but would be soon, the green stems a promise of beautiful things to come. Feeders were placed beside each plant,and several birds were taking advantage, munching on seeds. The residence wasn't as large as Kamden's but appeared to be well maintained, warm, and cozy.

The trip to the home had been amazing. Kamden had engaged her in conversation along the way, asking her things, providing answers when she turned the tables. He'd opened up to her, smiling and laughing freely, no longer confined by the cage that had trapped him for years. He'd touched her often, clasping her leg, holding her hand, shooting her looks that promised he had more in store for her.

A picture had eventually developed, winding around her heart. He wasn't the bastard she thought he was. He acted as he had as a defense mechanism, shoving people away. His hurt was real, causing him to fold in on himself. He didn't trust women, and she understood. He'd been injured in a way that had changed him, flipping him around and making him cold and distant, turning him into something different.

Those days were over.

She understood his lack of interest in the world and people, recalling how it was when her father had been diagnosed with terminal cancer. Although she couldn't see the danger, she knew it was there. She could feel pain and misery watching over her and her father. The blasted monster waited in the wings, eager to take what she loved from her, and she couldn't do anything about it. The only way to shield herself had been to turn to things she could control, giving her a sense of balance. She'd focused on herself and her dad, turning away from people, giving her hero all she could even if it wasn't enough.

It had worked until he died.

The first day without him showed her how lonely life could be.

Kamden opened the door behind hers, clucking his tongue as he instructed Baloo to jump down. Baloo did so right away, barking over and over, spinning in circles. Her door opened, and the man she'd somehow broken through to was right there. He hadn't pulled her crutches out of the back, meaning he wanted to carry her inside. That alone had her insides pooling, her legs growing weak. He handed her a key and reached out for her. She wrapped her arms around his neck, and he lifted her.

He buried his face into her neck, giving her throat a bite. "Got me, darlin'?"

"I've got you." *And I'm never letting you go.*

He hiked her up, pulling her from the seat, and closed the door with his hip. "How's the ankle?"

Since he'd told her to take pain medication hours ago, the pain was minimal. "It's good."

He crossed the distance quickly, taking her to the door. She slid the key into the lock, giving them unhindered passage, and he thrust the barrier aside.

She took in her surroundings, noting the furniture was dark and large like Kamden's. A leather couch was placed in the middle of the living room next to the fireplace. A spacious kitchen waited immediately to the right. Both areas were neat and tidy. He strode to the couch, bending at the waist, and lowered her to the furniture. She didn't let him go, maintaining a grip, not wanting him to move away. She thrust her nose into Kamden's chest, breathing him in. She didn't know what cologne he wore, but she liked it. Combined with his own unique and amazing scent, the fragrance went right to her head.

He chuckled, giving her a squeeze. "You naughty girl." He brought his head down, brushing his nose against hers. "I need to bring our things inside and let Baloo out back before I take you to lunch. You better decide what you want before I get back. If you don't, it's my choice."

With reluctance, she released her grip, eased back, and slid the key into his hand. "You know the area better than I do. It's probably for the best."

"It's up to you." He ran his fingers through her hair—something he liked to do whenever she was close—and breezed his lips over hers. "I'll be right back."

Kamden took Baloo to the back door, let him out, and went to the truck to get their things. She brought her foot up and rested it on the ottoman next to the couch. Her ankle was still sore, but between the medication and ice packs he'd brought along, the pain was tolerable. The only thing she didn't like was the grogginess. Reclining against the leather, she closed her eyes.

"I think we should order in," Kamden said, and she cracked an eye open. She watched him stroll inside and put his duffel, her backpack, and those vile crutches down. "You can rest until the food gets here."

"There are places that'll deliver here?" The house wasn't near town.

"They charge a fee, but it's worth it." He came over to her, plopped down beside her, and placed his hand on her thigh. "Did you decide what you want?"

A simple touch had her revving up. Why couldn't she get sex off her mind? She'd been aroused after their first encounter, wanting a repeat. "Is that a trick question?"

He got her intent, shifting toward her, but before he could take things further, his phone rang. When he moved away to see who was calling, she wanted to groan in frustration.

He looked at the screen, stood, and answered. "We just made it."

Aware it had to be Brady, she accepted her lot in life, leaning back and closing her eyes again. She heard Kamden go back outside, probably to get the things he'd left in the truck. Baloo rested his head on her leg, and she rubbed behind his ear. It was a good thing he wasn't as young as he used to be. He enjoyed long walks and hikes. When her ankle healed, she planned on making it up to him. She heard Kamden return, but she didn't open her eyes, staying as she was, trying to relax.

Firm hands gripped her waist, and she jolted upright.

Kamden bent at the waist, bringing them face-to-face. "Brady's going to bring you lunch. We'd better make this fast."

He kissed her hard, his tongue forceful as it flicked against hers, his fingers digging into her hips. Her heart pounded, her nipples straining against her bra. She moaned into his mouth, wrapping her arms around his neck. Her pussy clenched, her clit throbbing. A gush of wetness soaked her panties. She went from zero to sixty when he touched her.

He stepped back and helped flip her around, facing her toward the back of the couch. His hands wrapped around her stomach and went to work, undoing the button on her jeans and lowering the zipper. He tugged the fabric down to her knees, his hand smoothing over her ass before he reached between her legs and rubbed a finger through her folds.

"Damn, you're ready for me. I like that." He spread the moisture around, plunging two fingers into her. She arched her back, whimpering. "Oh yeah, you're ready. So am I." He let her go and leaned back. She heard him unzipping and lowering his jeans. "When we make it back tonight, there won't be any fucking in a hurry. I want to take my time with you." He slid on a condom and pressed against her, his cock gliding against her ass. His lips came to her ear, and he breathed into it. His tongue rasped over the outer shell, sending a shiver up her spine. "But until then, I'll take you however I can get you."

His hand pushed her forward, and she grasped the couch, resting her chest against the cushion. His cock prodded her sex, the broad head feeling more intimidating in this position. She stopped worrying when he eased in, discovering that the tight fit allowed him to stroke delicious places inside her. He slid his hands under her sweater and bra, his fingers surrounding and tweaking her nipples.

"Fuck, baby," he groaned, sinking the rest of the way in, "that's good."

It absolutely was. He felt so big behind her, trapping her in place, keeping her where he wanted her. His place was slow and smooth but became faster and harsher as he pumped his hips. He slipped his hands from her bra, placing one in her hair and the other over her clit. He turned her head, angling it to kiss her as he rubbed his fingers against the sensitive area. She timed herself, meeting his thrusts, driving him deeper into her. The tingles in her belly expanded like a current, trickling all over her body, heating it up.

He moved from her lips, nipping at her neck. "I want you to come, baby. I want to feel your tight little cunt clamping down on me." He intensified the movement and pressure of his fingers, and she whimpered. "That's it, sweetness. We'll take the edge off for now. Give it to me. Work me with that hot and tight little pussy."

God, the man liked to talk dirty. Another first for her.

Not that she was complaining.

He had no shame, which made her less inhibited, allowing her to let go of any shyness or embarrassment. She felt the hum inside her that warned an orgasm was close, a building pressure in her sex that was about to give him exactly what he wanted. Her breath caught, the intensity of it too much. She clutched the couch, bouncing on his cock, and tossed her head back as she came. It felt like a detonation, sex to the billionth power. She shook with the intensity of it, riding the pulsing waves, her pussy flexing and releasing.

"That's it. God, that's it." His voice changed, becoming harsh. His thrusts turned rough, his pace fast and frenzied. He brought his hands to her hips, his fingers digging into her skin. "That's my fucking girl."

He grunted, ramming into her a final time, and held her still. He rested his chest against her back, burying his face into the curve of her nape, and she felt a tremor go through him. His chest rose and fell as he panted, his fingers going lax. He wrapped his arm around her waist, resting his head on her shoulder, staying inside her.

"I don't think I'll ever get enough of you," he said with a heavy sigh.

Placing her hand on his arm, she said, "I hope not."

"You don't have to hope." Pressing a kiss to her neck, he pulled out of her, letting her go. "Wait right there."

She folded her arms on the couch, resting her head on them as he removed the condom, tossed it in the trash, and dressed. After taking Baloo back outside, he came to her, pulled up her jeans, and helped her with her clothes.

"Here you go." He brought the ottoman back, having kicked it aside at some point. His touch was gentle as he removed the boot and placed her leg on top of the furniture. "I'll get another ice pack."

There he went again, wanting to pamper her after sex. To her, it was the sweetest thing in the world. He seemed genuine in his concern, making sure she was seen to, wanting to look after her. She didn't argue, waiting as he did just that. When the ice was in place, he sat beside her, pulling her into his arms. She placed her head against his chest, getting situated.

"After you eat," he glided his fingers through her hair, making her scalp tingle, "I want you to lie down."

"What about you?" He'd only had breakfast. "Don't you need to eat?"

"I'll grab something on the way back. Bray got away early, and he has to get back before Candice knows he slipped out."

"Why is he coming here? Wouldn't it be faster to meet him?"

"We're taking my truck in case they cross paths."

"All right." A nap would definitely help, giving the drugs time to get out of her system. She wasn't taking more of them unless she had to. "I can sleep on the couch. It's comfortable enough. I just need a pillow and the crutches if I need to hit the bathroom."

"I think I can make that happen."

Minutes passed in silence, their breathing the only sound in the room. He kept petting her, combing his fingers through her hair, caressing her back. She luxuriated in his touch, finding it comforting and relaxing. When the front door opened, she wondered if Kamden would pull away. He didn't, remaining as he was.

She turned slightly to see the man of the hour.

Her eyes bulged when her attention swept to Brady. He looked like his brother with dark hair and brown eyes, but where Kamden was lean and muscular from physical labor, Brady devoted serious time to the gym. He looked as tall as Kamden too. The man was freaking enormous.

"Delivery service," he said with a grin, placing the bag in his hand on the ottoman.

"Let me get her settled, and we'll go." Kamden slipped his arms away and rose, leaving her alone with this sibling.

"Everly, right?" She nodded and he said, "I'm Brady." He extended a hand, and she offered him hers, thinking he was going to shake it. Instead, he bowed at the waist, bringing her hand to his lips, pressing a soft kiss against her knuckles. He let her go and smiled, taking him from intimidating to charming. "It's nice to meet you."

Damn. No wonder Candice fell hard.

Any woman would.

His gaze landed on her ankle, and he cringed. "Kam said you got hurt. I hope it's not bothering you too much."

"It's more annoying than anything."

She heard the sliding glass door open, and Kamden said, "I'm letting Baloo in. He's had time to do his business."

"All right." She'd rest easier if he was nearby.

The dog came into the room, prancing and wagging his tail. Brady grinned, kneeling down. "Hey, boy. You are a big one, aren't you?" He ran his fingers over Baloo's head, glancing at Kamden. "Almost as big as a pony."

"Just don't try to get on him and take a ride," Kamden joked, laughing. He placed a pillow and blanket beside her. Then he went to get her crutches. "Your big ass will break his back."

"How did you manage to get your hands on a Swiss mountain dog?" Brady continued petting Baloo. "They're pretty rare around these parts."

"Dad worked for a couple that bred them. He gave me Baloo on my birthday."

Brady gave Baloo one final pat and stood. "He's beautiful."

"Thank you."

"You ready?" Kam pulled out his keys.

Brady's chocolate brown gaze landed on her. "Are you going to be all right?"

"I'll be fine." The man wore his heart on his sleeve, and the concern on his face made her smile. Wanting to reassure him, she revealed her plans. "I'm going to eat and take a nap."

He frowned like he didn't believe her.

After a moment, he went into the kitchen and brought a folding table over. He put it beside her, retrieved the bag with the lunch he'd brought, and set it all out for her. Then he went back to the kitchen and returned with a phone. Kamden watched with a grin on his face as though he expected everything to play out as it did.

"Here you go." Brady put the phone on the table. "Call if something changes."

Not only was he gorgeous, he was protective.

"I will." She opened the plastic container and saw he'd brought her burritos with rice and beans. She pulled her utensils from the plastic package. "Thank you for lunch. You boys be good."

"I'll get him back to you on one piece."

They left the house, locking the door behind them. She hadn't asked to go with them. Brady was about to buy something that would change his life. It was personal, private, and should be shared with someone he knew and trusted. She wondered how that felt, to have a sibling you grew up with. She wouldn't know anything about that. Her mother had reached out a few years ago after her father had gotten his diagnosis, saying her half-sister wanted to meet and talk with her. She'd declined, not wanting anything to do with that side of her family.

She'd considered reaching out here and there but never did.

Sometimes ignorance was bliss.

"You said she was young and attractive, but you didn't

tell me she was *that* young and attractive." Brady looked at his brother, observing him closely. As much as he wanted Kam to move on with his life, he didn't want an innocent girl to get hurt if things didn't work out. He hadn't expected her to be in her early twenties, thinking she was a few years older. She still had innocence in her eyes, something that many women lost along the way. Candice certainly had until he'd found her, loved her, and turned things around. "She's already fallen for you. You can see it in the way she looks at you."

"My intentions are honorable, Bray." Kamden turned on the road that led to town. "I tried to leave her alone, but she decided to put her foot down. I talked to her like she asked me to, and things progressed from there. I wasn't the one who took things to the next level, not until I was asked. I'm not going to fuck her and leave her if that's what you're worried about."

"I'm not trying to piss you off," Brady said slowly, not wanting to stir up shit if he didn't have to. Regardless, certain things had to be said. "You brought her with you. That says a lot about how you feel. But you knew as soon as I saw her, I'd bring this up."

"I brought up the age difference. She doesn't care."

"That's good." And it was. Brady didn't have a lot of room to talk. He did kinky shit that some people might consider wrong or perverted. "If you're both fine with it, that's all that matters." He hesitated because that wasn't enough. There was more he needed to put out there and get in the open.

"You want to say something," Kamden grumbled, "so say it."

"She's young, and you've been through a lot of shit. I don't know if that's a good or bad thing. I'm just trying to understand what's going on. The last time we talked, you said you didn't want to have anything to do with her. Now she's here with you. It's thrown me off. I don't want either of you to get hurt."

Kamden glanced over. "Are you worried about her or me?"

"I think the answer is obvious. I'm worried about both of you."

"I've talked to her. We have an understanding."

That was good, but he needed to hear more. "What kind of understanding?"

"We're giving each other a chance."

There was one way to know if that was true. "Are you going to tell Mom and Dad?"

That pissed Kamden off. His knuckles turned white as he fisted the steering wheel. "I'm not going to be keeping secrets, if that's what you mean. I'm not going to be hiding her when guests come by."

"When I visit with Candice, I can expect to see you and Everly at Sunday dinner?"

Kamden eased his grip on the wheel, calming down. "I'm going to tell them, Bray. Things have happened in a couple of days, and I haven't had a chance. To answer your question, yes, you will see us there. I just have to figure out when and where. They'll crowd Everly once they know. I don't think she understands that yet, and I don't want to push her before she's ready."

"Mom and Dad will be over the moon." He decided to redirect the conversation. If his brother and Everly had an understanding, they both knew the rewards and risks of getting involved with each other. They were consenting adults. There wasn't anything he could do about that. "They're going to drive both of us crazy."

Kam chuckled, nodding. "No babies in the near future for you?"

"No. I'm a selfish bastard and want Candice all to myself. We've talked about it, and she wants children, so it'll happen eventually." He grinned, wondering what his older sibling had in store. "What about you?"

"I'm not the one getting married, at least not yet."

"I want you to be my best man." They'd always said they would be if and when the time came. When Kamden had proposed to Delaney, he'd asked Brady to do the same. "What do you say?"

"Of course. So when's the wedding?"

"That'll be up to her." A surge of worry overcame him, reminding him things were moving incredibly fast. "If she says yes."

"Have you been loving the hell out of her like I told you to?"

And then some. "I have."

"Then she'll say yes. Just make sure you get a ring she can't refuse."

Fuck. The Ring. There were so many options. He didn't know where to start. "I thought about getting her something big and fancy, but that's not her style. I think unique is best."

"If that's what you think, then you're probably right. Get her something that reminds you of her. Make sure you tell her that when you propose." Kamden looked at him, meeting his eyes. "When are you proposing, anyway?"

"In Florida. I'm not sure when. I want us to be alone when it happens."

"That's smart. Mom and Dad will hound the two of you if they see a ring while you visit." Kamden's tone softened, "When the moment comes, you'll know when the time's right."

"We'll see."

They drove the rest of the way, making idle chatter, and Brady didn't bring up Everly or ask any questions about her. Still, he worried how things would go. Kamden had never been mean or spiteful in his youth, but he'd developed the traits after his heart had been broken. This was the first time he'd put himself out there, actually sticking around and caring for a woman instead of thinking with his dick. Brady hoped the young girl with flowing hair, shining hazel eyes, and a radiant smile could get through to his brother without getting hurt in the process.

If she'd gotten this far, maybe they *could* give each other a chance.

For both their sakes, he hoped so.

CHAPTER EIGHT

EVERLY GAZED AROUND, thinking the restaurant they'd come to was cozy but also odd. One side was for the fine dining, the other was for dancing, and the back room was set up with billiard tables and dartboards. For a Monday, the place was busy enough.

There was something for everyone.

Her focus shot to Kamden, and she drank him up, devouring him with her eyes. He'd changed into clothing she'd never seen him in before, donning a dress shirt, slacks, and nice shoes. She brushed her hair with her fingers and swiped her fingers under her eyes. She hadn't gone overboard with makeup, but she'd taken care with her appearance, changing into a nicer sweater and jeans. Candice and Brady were set to arrive at any minute, and she wanted to make a good impression.

"I'm getting you on that floor before we go," Kamden warned, sliding the hand on her thigh upward so his pinkie brushed her sex. "I want a slow song with you."

She moved the table cloth aside, waving at her foot. "I can't walk, much less dance."

"I'll get you there."

She was sure he could if she'd let him. "You're not carrying me in here."

"No one will know, darlin'. I'll help you stand up, put an arm around you, and you can pretend to glide."

"Aren't you tired of carrying me around?"

"Not one bit. Are you?"

She liked it, actually. "As long as it's not in front of God and the world."

He laughed and grasped the beer he'd ordered. She mirrored him, drinking her cocktail. Kamden had found the entire process of ordering humorous while she'd been annoyed. When the server had asked for identification, he cocked a brow, taking her back to when he'd brought up the difference in their ages. Personally, she didn't think it was that big a damned deal.

"So that's what she looks like," Kamden said softly. "Now it all makes sense."

Her gaze darted up, and she saw Brady approaching. His arm was snaked around the waist of a curvy blonde with the biggest blue eyes she'd ever seen. She dressed to show off her body, highlighting her bust and flared waist. As concerned as Brady had been when they'd met, he was all grins now, his attention centered on the woman he obviously loved. Since he'd took time with his appearance as well, they both stood out, drawing stares from nearby tables.

Kamden eased his hand from her thigh and stood. "It's about time."

Brady grinned and made introductions. "Candice, this is my brother Kamden." Candice shook Kamden's hand, giving him a smile. "And this is Everly." She let Kamden go and turned to Everly, still smiling as she repeated the motions.

"It's nice to meet you both."

Brady pulled out her chair. "Here you go, baby."

As soon as she was seated, he took the place beside her. The pair were extremely hands-on, getting as close to each other as possible.

"Old Man Foster really worked on the place," Kamden said, snagging his beer. He placed his hand on her thigh again, running his thumb back and forth over the denim. "The pool area didn't exist the last time I was here."

"He's improved things over the years," Brady replied. "The tables in the back run fast, but they're level if you want to play a game."

The waiter returned. Since they'd arrived early, Everly and Kamden had already given their orders. Apparently, Candice and Brady frequented the place. They indicated what they wanted without looking at the menu. As the waiter scurried off, Everly lowered her hand and placed it over Kamden's, trying to steady her nerves.

He didn't know how she felt about these kinds of things.

She always struggled in crowded places, finding it hard to breathe. She'd never been good in social situations since they made her apprehensive. She preferred an evening at home rather than one spent out and about. Since she was determined to prove she was mature enough to handle things with him, she had to grin and bear it. With her heart racing and panic rising, she thought she should have shared her anxieties before they came to a place like this.

"So Everly," Candice said, her lovely smile still in place, her sapphire blue eyes shining, "what do you do?"

"Restore and flip houses," she answered, trying to relax. She studied the stunning woman across from her. "How about yourself?"

"Nothing nearly as crafty as that. I'm a reporter."

No wonder she seemed so confident. "That sounds interesting."

"It can be, sometimes." Candice sighed, and her smile faded. "Unless you're working on boring things, which I've been relegated to." Her gaze to flickered to Brady, who only had eyes for her. "My boss wasn't pleased when I told him I was going on vacation. He's put me on menial things until I come back."

"Menial in what way?"

"I've been doing the rounds on gardening and upcoming Farmer's Markets. It's about as exciting as watching paint dry."

"I suppose it's a good thing I'm my own boss."

"I guess it is." Candice studied her for a moment. "Isn't it difficult?"

"Which part?" She picked up her drink and took a sip.

"The planning, along with the lifting and moving."

Ah, there it was. The woman thought she would blow over with a stiff breeze. "I've been doing it since I was ten. I'm stronger than I look."

"I believe that." The curiosity in Candice's gaze changed to appreciation. "I tip my hat to you. I know I wouldn't be able to do it."

The waiter brought Candice and Brady's drinks and indicated the food would arrive soon. As he left, a melody carried from the dance floor. They'd seen the sign on the door stating music started at eight o'clock. Several of the couples seated at the bar rose and went to the area.

"The two of you would work well together, then," Brady said, shifting his attention to Everly and Kamden. "She could restore while you build."

"What do you think about that, darlin'?" Kamden asked, a devilish light in his whiskey-colored eyes. "Think we can find a place that fits the bill?"

She snorted because there already was one. "I have to finish my place first."

"The Wilson property, right?" Brady questioned, giving her a grin. "It's been a few years, but it was in rough shape when I stopped by. Frank got too old to take care of it."

"It belonged to her great-grandparents, actually," Kamden said, his gaze flickering to her, pride evident in his features. "When you visit, you need to stop by. She's redone the floors, walls, and installed crown molding. You'll be amazed at everything she's changed."

"Really?" Brady focused on her again. "I thought it

would have to be gutted."

"Nothing so severe as that on the inside, just a lot of elbow grease, time, and love. A few of the floorboards had to be replaced, but it wasn't too bad. The exterior might pose a problem, but it's sound for now." She thought about the barn and property, which were another matter. "I'll have to hire someone to cut the trees, mow down the grass, and demolish the barn. I'm amazed it hasn't caved in on itself by now."

"You don't have to hire shit," Kamden corrected her right away, flipping his hand to twine his fingers with hers. "Say when, and I'll take care of it."

She started to respond when Brady stopped her. "He can do the exterior and roof too. Don't let him hold back on you. He has one of the best crews in Alabama and comes to Tennessee all the time because people know how good he is. He can take care of your problems in a few days. I'd make him earn his keep if I were you."

Something struck her, and it meant the world to her. They all picked up on her anxiety and wanted to alleviate it, keeping her engaged in conversation, trying to put her at ease. That alone allowed her to take a moment and really breathe. She was surrounded by strangers, but friends sat directly across from her.

She didn't need to put on a mask in front of them.

They saw and accepted her for who she was.

Kamden was grateful to Candice and Brady. They'd sensed Everly's tension as much as he had. Together they'd worked to remedy it. They'd kept her mind on things that allowed her to come out of her shell, ensuring she remained calm, giving her all the time she needed.

"You heard your brother. When you have the time," Everly said, leaning against Kamden, meeting his gaze, "fix the problem."

He didn't give a shit if anyone saw what he was about to do, ready to grasp her by the nape and kiss the ever-loving hell out of her. Brady had brought up honest questions when they'd gone to buy a ring. Seeing Everly in this place, discovering how insecure she could be even if she tried to hide it, allowed Kamden to see the youthfulness she retained. No wonder Brady had been worried. She had to be handled with delicate care, treated as a treasure.

Before he could follow through with the kiss, a voice from his past intruded. "Kammie, is that you?"

It felt like he'd been doused in freezing water, so icy and cold it seeped into his bones. There was only one person who used that name. He had to turn from Everly to find the source of the question. It felt like everything slowed down, his heart sinking to his stomach. When his gaze landed on the only woman he'd ever loved, he didn't know if he should stand up and treat her like the princess he used to or run to the nearest bathroom to vomit.

Time had changed her, but not overly much. Delaney had a few fine lines around her doe brown eyes, and she'd dyed her blonde hair red. She was as fit and trim as he remembered, built like a gazelle with legs that went on for days. He noted she hadn't changed the way she dressed, wearing a top and skirt that revealed a hint of her tummy, her heels bringing those long limbs into focus.

"It's me," he finally said, meeting her gaze. "Hello, Delaney."

They hadn't spoken in years. She'd tried to reach out to him on numerous occasions, telling him she wanted to explain and talk to him. He'd blown her off, not willing to listen. She'd known how he was, but she hadn't given a shit.

What were the odds that she'd be here now?

I have the worst fucking luck.

"I thought it was." She glanced at Everly. Then her attention centered on him. Hiking her chin in the direction of the bar, she asked, "Can I borrow you for a minute?"

In normal circumstances, he'd have told her to fuck off.

Then he felt the fingers resting against his.

He didn't want Everly anywhere near the heinous bitch.

The woman he'd brought with him was pure, sweet, and undefiled by the world. He wouldn't shame her with Delaney's presence and felt somewhat sick even thinking about it. At that moment, he truly understood his brother's concern. Kamden had been distant and cold, running from what he couldn't handle. If he wanted to get past that, he had to face the demons in his past once and for all. Once he was done, Delaney would understand how things were now. He released the hand in his, ready to get this shit over with once and for all.

"Excuse me," he told everyone at the table, both angry and relieved he could close this chapter in his life. "I'll be right back."

He caught Brady's shocked expression, then his furious glare. He knew where it came from. Brady wanted to protect Everly and would do everything he could to shelter her. He thought Kamden should address his ex in front of everyone. Despite that, Kamden disregarded it, accepting this was something he had to do. He wasn't going to go anywhere with his former love and would return to Everly's side in a matter of minutes.

To let go of things, he had to truly let them go.

Perhaps it was serendipity or some higher power showing him a sign.

No matter what it was, he had to get this over and done with.

It was time.

He followed Delaney, winding through tables and chairs in their paths, going around the curve of the bar. Delaney took them to a place they wouldn't be seen, turning only when they made it there. She hesitated for a moment, and they sized each other up. They were former lovers who didn't know each other anymore.

She wasn't as beautiful as he once found her and paled in comparison to the youthful girl who giggled and played with him in the shower earlier in the day. In truth, he and Delaney hadn't had much in common. He was simple, wanting to save, looking ahead. She lived in the moment, liked nice things, and complained when she didn't get them. While he'd done everything he could for her, busting his ass, she'd decided it wasn't good enough. She not only wanted him to take care of her, she wanted to do whatever the fuck she wanted in between.

"It's been a long time," she said softly, her eyes roaming over his body. That kind of look turned him on before, getting him hard and ready. Now it just made him feel physically ill.

"Not long enough," he grated, leaning against the counter. "What do you want?"

"You never understood me," she said, but there was no venom in her voice, only resolve. "Not when we actually grew up. You made me out to be the bad guy. You never wanted to see your part in things. It wasn't and isn't fair."

So she wants to blame me.

"I wasn't the one who fucked around," he reminded her.

She absorbed that and nodded. "I know, but you were part of the problem. You are the reason I strayed." He started to speak, but she stopped him, continuing, "I never saw you. If you weren't working, you were at school. I had to stay at home by myself day after day. I couldn't do it anymore. I told you I needed my own life. You didn't listen, and I got lonely."

"Well," he said, envisioning her in his bed with Josh, "you found a way to take care of that, didn't you?"

"You still think I'm responsible for what happened?"

Is she fucking serious?

Ire stirred, and he prepared to give her hell. Then he remembered what Everly had said.

If Delaney had such an issue, she could have told him they needed to talk. She could have tried to explain things. That's what normal people did. Delaney could have come to him, and he would have listened. For whatever reason, she hadn't done so.

"Actually, yes. I do. You could have told me what bothered you before you decided to fuck around."

"I was a kid, Kamden. We both were." Her temper sparked, something he remembered very well, and she put her hands on her hips. "I was young and stupid."

The fact came from her lips, not his. "If you say so."

She sighed, shaking her head. "I'm not trying to interfere in your life. Too much time has gone by. I just wanted to talk to you since you never gave me a chance. I just want you to know I'm sorry. I made a mistake, and you got hurt. So did Josh. We were impulsive and did something we shouldn't have. You should know he regrets it as much—if not more—than I do. We didn't mean to hurt you. It just happened. Then you wouldn't give us a chance to talk to you. You packed up and left. You wouldn't even return our calls."

He found himself wanting to return to Everly.

He wanted to hear her laughter and see her smile.

He remembered coming to Sunday dinner with his parents and meeting her the first time, finding himself attracted to her even if he didn't want to be. It hadn't merely been her looks but the energy around her. She was vibrant, full of life, eager to laugh and smile. She reminded him of a child at the first circus, taking everything in, wanting to see what came next.

Then he thought about how much she'd lost.

From their conversations, she'd had one person in her world. That man was long gone, leaving her on her own.

She'd endured more than anyone should, but she came through the other side, maintaining her wit, humanity, and love for others. Somehow, some fucking way, she'd latched on to his worthless ass and brought him back to the person he used to be. She'd made him optimistic even if he didn't think he could be.

He'd known as soon as he'd been introduced to her that she was too good for him, full of life and vibrancy. They'd only spent a couple of days together, but she'd already got into his system like a drug, creating a drive to take more of her energy and spirit into himself.

As that notion came to him, the anger and hurt faded.

Sometimes bad things were a blessing in disguise.

The one-night stands and years shielding himself had made him a complete and total bastard. He didn't want to be the idiot he'd become, eager to forge a new path, wanting to move on. He envisioned Everly on the drive up, picturing her cheeky grin as she'd handed him snacks and reached back to pet Baloo, showing him her true self even when he was afraid to do the same. He recalled how her jovial nature made his steely exterior crumble and fade. She'd made him a better person in a matter of hours, showing him that life carried on.

She'd accepted him without pause, wanting to know him.

Even though he hadn't deserved it.

"It was a long time ago," he finally admitted, letting the influence of the woman who'd come into his life wash over him. "If you hadn't done what you did, I wouldn't have met the woman I came here with. She wouldn't be in my life." He couldn't believe he was about to say it, but he did, "I suppose I should thank you for that. I wouldn't have her if it wasn't for you."

"Do you love her?"

He was well on his way.

Only he hadn't realized it until that moment.

He wanted to spend all his time with Everly Mason, the hardest worker he'd ever met, the most giving soul he'd ever encountered. He wanted to see that impish grin she gave him, listening as she laughed and said silly things. He'd only been with her a short time, but he knew it wasn't nearly enough for him. If she'd let him, he'd chain her to his side, knowing each day when he went to work, he'd come home to find her waiting for him.

"Yes," he said, realizing it could happen just like that.

After all, it was how it had been with the woman in front of him.

He saw the way Delaney's gaze dropped and realized she'd hoped she could reconnect with him. That would never happen. Not in this lifetime. Especially with the young woman he had waiting for him just around the corner.

"I'm happy for you," she said but didn't seem to be.

Instead of fury, he felt relief so strong he wanted to drop to his knees. He meant what he said, swamped by the emotions flowing through him. He met her gaze, needing to tell her something, meaning every single word. "I'm not mad at you anymore. I'm grateful. Thank you for doing what you did and giving her to me." He let his eyes hover over the girl-turned-woman he once loved, ready to let her go. "Take care of yourself, Laney."

He spun around, a spring in his step, leaving the horrid shit behind him. He was in new territory, but he wasn't afraid. Not anymore. Everly had said she wanted a chance like he did. He wanted to take advantage of that.

When he came around, searching for and finding his table, he frowned. Candice and Everly were gone. Only Brady remained at the table, and he looked furious. He hurried over, worried as Everly shouldn't be on her bad ankle, when his brother rose and faced him.

"Where are the girls?" he asked, glancing around.

"They're gone," Brady informed him, rising from his

seat, his voice vibrating with heavy emotion. "Really, Kam? She was already nervous and edgy. You had to do that to her?"

"What did I do?" He intended to do right by Everly, wanting her to know she was the one he wanted. He panicked when the words really sank in, and he noticed cash on the table. "What do you mean they're gone?"

"You ditched her for Delaney, *Kammie*," Brady mocked, visibly angry. "Did you think she wouldn't know who the fuck came up the table, Kam? The minute you walked away, her guard went up. She's young, but she's not stupid." Brady tossed money on the table, covering the bill. "And you went right along with the bitch without so much as an introduction or look back, like a fucking asshole that can't see what's right in front of him."

"I didn't want her anywhere near Everly." His temper stirred because his brother had it all wrong. "I went to talk to her because I'm ready to move on. I'm tired of all the bullshit." He faced his sibling, meeting his gaze. "I want to start living my own life, Bray. I'm ready to let it all go."

His brother's expression changed, turning less harsh, softening as he finally got the fucking memo. "I'm supposed to take you to the apartment with me. When you left, Everly marched out of here on that bum leg of hers. Candice went with her and calmed her down. She's taking Everly to get her things and Baloo." Brady exhaled softly. "Everly wants to go home, Kam."

Fuck that.

"I'm going to her."

Brady lowered his head and warned, "You'll have to get through me first."

"Are you shitting me?" he snarled, readying to rip his brother a new asshole. "You're willing to fight me over this?"

"I'm willing to fight you because Everly is upset,"

Brady corrected him. "She doesn't want you there. She wants to go home and nurse her wounds." His younger sibling took a deep breath, placing his hands on the table. "I asked you those questions before because I saw the light in her eyes. She's just a girl who wants to be loved, but I don't have to tell you that, do I?" His gaze drifted up, and his brown eyes had turned black. "You might have had your reasons, but you snuffed that glow out in seconds. She lit out of here like a fire was on her ass."

Full-fledged alarm sank in, and he prepared to leave.

Brady came over and snatched his arm. "If you mean what you just said, give her space. Candice told me she broke down outside. She can't even talk right now. If you care about her, you have to get your shit together and give her space. You told me if I didn't want to hurt Candice, I had to love the hell of her. If you want to love the hell out of the one you want, you have to back off right now and let her breathe. Going to her now won't help either of you. She's not in the mood to listen to you."

He didn't know what to do.

"Candice will watch over her, Kam. I'll call her and explain. She'll talk to Everly. Give her time to smooth things out."

"I just wanted it over with." That was the honest truth. "I didn't want Delaney to taint what I have now. I wanted to listen to her once and for all and move on with my life." He did something he never had before, pleading with his brother. "Please, Brady. I didn't mean any harm. It was entirely the opposite. I wasn't thinking about anything but getting the shit over with." Hoping he could convey that, meeting his brother's torn stare, he said, "I need to go to her. Especially if she's hurt."

"Shit, Kam." Brady drew a deep breath and dropped the hand he'd placed on Kamden's forearm. "You're going to have your hands full. Everly's upset with you, and Candice wants your balls."

"You take care of yours, and I'll take care of mine." He retrieved his keys. "Are we going?"

"We'll go, but you should know this, big brother." Brady got up in his business. "You hurt that girl, and we're going to have a problem."

"I'm not going to." Kamden didn't get angry, aware that Brady always tried to protect women. "She needs to know what I said to Delaney. She needs to know she made it all possible."

He didn't wait for permission, stepping around his brother, hurrying for the door.

He'd never hurt Everly, not ever again.

CHAPTER NINE

EVERLY TRIED TO stop shaking as she removed her things from Kamden's duffel and placed them in the luggage Candice provided. She couldn't believe he'd gone off with the woman who'd broken his heart. She'd kept it together, believing he had a reason, until something crept into her mind and refused to budge. Her insecurities laughed at and mocked her, informing her there was a very good reason he'd left her side to speak to his former flame.

Kamden was still in love with the leggy redhead.

That was the reason he'd avoided relationships. He couldn't be in one because he already knew who he wanted. He might have instigated the breakup, but he obviously had second thoughts.

The entire situation reminded her of her mother.

When Everly turned five, Gloria had shown up with her new husband Luther. She tried to establish contact, telling Everly she'd have a brother or sister soon. Everly had shoved her away, locked herself in her room, and told her father she wanted nothing to do with the woman. The only good thing her mother had ever done was to respect that wish.

I'm so fucking stupid.

"Let me," Candice stepped in, motioning to the couch.

Everly shook her head, not wanting to cry again. "I've got it."

"I know you do, but I want to help." Candice placed

her hand over Everly's. "I was your age when someone hurt me, Everly. The situations are different, but pain and humiliation are universal. I've been where you are. I know how it feels."

"No one should feel like this." *Ever.*

"I know," Candice said softly. "He's a dick. Fuck him."

Caving in, Everly turned and sat on the couch. Baloo was right there, sensing her pain, wanting to alleviate it. She reached down, sliding her fingers around his neck. He brought his big head up, nudging her chin. The dog had been a constant in her life. If she'd been smart, she would have kept it that way. She was like millions of delusional women across the world who met men and thought they had what it took to get through to them.

She just wanted to go home and pull herself together.

It wouldn't be easy, as the reminder of her stupidity lived right beside her.

Maybe it was best to go with plan two. She could fix up the place, put it on the market, and move on. There were several properties she'd looked at before she'd decided to carve a place for herself at the home her father once visited as a child. She had enough money to buy another property and fix it up. If and when the house she'd been working on sold, she could take a look at her finances and decide what she wanted to do next.

Lights came through the window, and she froze.

Candice pulled away, whipping around. She noted the lights that turned off and glanced at Everly with fury in her eyes. "Don't worry about a thing. I'll take care of it."

The fiery blonde stormed to the door, opened it, stepped outside, and closed it behind her. Everly discovered Brady and Candice had one thing in common. Both were exceptional at reading people. They protected those in their care and wouldn't let anything fuck with them. It was the first time she'd seen that kind of dynamic in a couple. The pair were on another wavelength, observing and understanding things on a unique and personal level, inserting themselves into situations when they felt they needed to.

When she'd risen from her seat, grasped the crutches, and tucked them under her arm, they'd gazed at each other, and a silent communication had taken place. It shouldn't have been possible, but they'd gotten on the same page right away and worked together as a unit. When Candice had followed her out, Brady had stayed where he was. After Candice had calmed her down, helping her muddle through tears and emotion, she'd asked Everly what she wanted to do. Everly informed her that she just wanted to go home. Candice told her to stay put and went back inside. The blonde returned with Brady's keys, telling her she'd drive her to the house to get her things.

They'd reacted without hesitation, rushing to take care of her.

If only Kamden could be like that.

The thought made the hurt worse. He'd been attentive with her when they'd been together, making sure she was comfortable, going out of his way to look after her. Now that he had what he really wanted, he'd tossed her aside like a useless toy. Reminded of that, she stood, welcoming the pain that shot through her leg when she put weight on it. She finished gathering her things, tossing them into the suitcase Candice had pulled from the closet.

She heard the door open and moved faster, eager to get home. Candice indicated Brady would drop Kamden off at her apartment and drive her back. She wanted to get back to her shoddy couch in her dismal and crowded trailer as soon as possible.

"Everly," Kamden's soft voice echoed in her ears. "I know how things look, but it's not what you think. I need to talk to you. I have to explain."

She didn't know why Brady had changed the game,

and she didn't really care. Kamden told her things weren't what she thought before, and she'd listened. Look where that had gotten her.

Left alone at a table while he went to talk to the first girl he'd ever loved.

Discarded like a plaything.

"Don't bother. I gave you a chance, and you blew it. I'm going home."

"No, you're not. Not until you hear me out," he said, coming around the other side of the couch. He wanted her to look at him, so she averted her eyes, keeping her attention on the task at hand. He noticed but didn't reach out or try to touch her. A very good thing, since she wanted to pummel him. "I did things in the wrong way. I do apologize for that."

Wow, really? "If you feel better now, can I go?"

"I'm not done." He sounded like he wanted to tear something apart. "I actually thanked the bitch. Do you know why?"

"Because she came back to you?"

His hand shot out, and he grasped her wrist. She looked up then, narrowing her eyes, wanting to vent her outrage at him. "Let me go before I slap the hell out of you."

He leaned over the couch undeterred, coming toward her. "What she did brought me to you. You wouldn't be in my life if she was still a part of it."

"I don't believe you." She wouldn't do so again. She only gave free passes once. Her mind drifted back to the image of him rising from the table and leaving her alone. She'd never felt more mortified. "Nothing you say will change that. It was fun but not *that* fun." Kamden hesitated, obviously shocked by her vehement reaction. It made sense. She kept this part of herself away from others, knowing how ugly it made her. "Didn't expect that, did you? You thought I'd go right along with things: Newsflash, dick. You have age on me, but not experience. I'll up the game and show you what misery truly feels like." Full of pain and grief, letting it flow through her, she snarled, "I've got news for you, *darlin'*. I wasn't feeding you bullshit like you did me. I've been through things you can't begin to comprehend. This isn't a blip on my radar."

She didn't back down, showing him a part of her she only reserved for people she truly hated, becoming the woman she had to be when he father passed. She leaned forward herself, looking him in the eye. "I'm done with you. You can't pass go, and you will never collect your two hundred dollars. You will leave me alone, or you'll regret meeting me."

He looked frantic, his eyes widening in alarm. "Everly, please."

No, she wouldn't please him. *Not again.*

"Back up."

He didn't listen, coming closer.

She clucked her tongue, wanting this over and done, and issued the order that took her dog from friendly to violent. "Guard."

She didn't use it often, so the large animal responded immediately.

Baloo, who was always sweet and calm, came to her side. He wasn't meant for this kind of work, but he'd taken to it like a duck to water. She hadn't expected it when she'd brought him to a trainer who showed her how to make things happen. Even her father had been surprised. The breed was known for its friendliness and patience, a renowned family pet. For some reason, Baloo was the exception to the rule, eager and willing to take care of her. It was one of many reasons she always kept him by her side.

The dog growled, baring its teeth, hiking its tail.

"I'll send him after you if you don't let me go." She didn't break the eye contact, wanting Kamden to know she meant it. "I mean it, *Kammie*," she sneered, a tendril of revulsion going down her spine as she recalled Delaney addressing Kamden as such. "Back off, or things are about to get nasty."

He reluctantly did so, easing away.

Excellent.

"Either you give me your keys, or I'm calling a cab. I'm going home, and I don't want to see you anywhere near my property. If you so much as put a foot on my land, you'll regret it. I have a gun, and I know how to use it." Seeing his bewildered state gave her a measure of peace. She didn't need Candice or Brady for this. She'd been underestimated much of her life, treated like some fragile thing that would wither and die without help. How little people knew. In their brief time together, she'd revealed the good that hid the bad. He had no idea what she was capable of. "You aren't allowed to be near me. Not now, and not ever again. You stay the fuck away from me."

He must have accepted she meant it because he pulled the keys from his slacks. He studied them for a moment, a look of confusion and agony on his face, and placed them on the cushioned back of the couch.

"I want to explain," he said quietly. "You owe me that."

"I don't owe you a damned thing. You got your piece of ass." She didn't give a shit, not wanting to hear a single word, taking the keys. "Your wants have no place here."

Since she had her things in the rolling luggage Candice had given her, it was time to go. She hiked the suitcase off the couch, pulled out the handle, and turned to go out the door. She didn't look back as she snatched her crutches and went to the porch, noting Candice and Brady hadn't left. They watched her as she tossed her things in the back of the vehicle. She didn't address either of them since they were Kamden's family, not hers.

They'd never see or talk to her again.

She snapped her fingers, and Baloo jumped inside, settling in the passenger seat. Her ankle throbbed miserably, but she didn't care. She put the keys in the ignition, fired up the engine, and put the truck in reverse to back out of the drive. She hit the road and drove, not looking back, trembling as she tried to settle down.

Once she made it home, she'd decide what to do next.

Kamden stood in the doorway to the house, watching Everly go. He couldn't believe she'd turned so quickly, going from sweet and innocent to harsh and livid. He'd never thought she had it in her, becoming something he'd never expected. She meant it when she'd told him she had misery inside her he'd never understand.

He heard it in her voice and saw it in her face.

Even the dog had changed its colors.

As obedient as the large animal had been, it turned on a dime with a simple word, revealing its teeth as its hackles raised. He'd been alarmed, watching the girl and dog he'd brought along with him to his brother's home turn into something he'd never anticipated. His heart felt heavy, his gut churning.

Just like that, she was gone.

Her words came back to him.

I'm done with you.

You stay the fuck away from me

She meant it, wanting nothing to do with him.

His gaze drifted from his truck as it hit the main road and vanished, landing on Candice and Brady. Both were watching him with concerned expressions. Fuck. What did he do now? He was shaken and off-balance, put in his proper fucking place. He'd fucked things good and hard, drawing a line in the sand even though he hadn't meant to. The only reason he'd let her go was the pain etched in her face. The outrage directed directly at him wasn't something he ever expected from her.

"What happened?" Brady finally asked, moving from

Candice.

"She's going home," he answered, bewildered that things had changed so quickly. "She's done."

"Done with what?" His brother studied him, no longer angry but worried.

It wasn't easy to admit, but he answered, "With me."

He pivoted and went back into the house, going to the couch. As he sank into the cushions covered by leather, he saw the coat she'd left behind. He grasped it and pulled it against him. He heard Brady and Candice coming inside, but he ignored them, trapped in his own thoughts and musings.

Was there a way to make it right?

Even if he could, would she listen?

Both things were highly doubtful.

He remained in a stunned state, wondering if he'd landed in a bad fucking dream. Things didn't happen like this in the real world. Or did they? He didn't have the experience to know for sure. All he did know was Everly wanted nothing to do with him. She'd make that crystal fucking clear. As he recalled her words, he winced because it was true.

You got your piece of ass.

He'd gone about things all wrong, but he hadn't meant to. She'd come at him like a woman who knew exactly what she wanted. For that reason, he'd reacted in turn, behaving as he always had. He'd tried to show her the sex wasn't all there was to it, but he hadn't offered pretty words or praise. He'd delved to his mental filing cabinet, offering her terms that felt right at the time. But she wasn't like the women who wanted sex and nothing more, wiping their hands after they were done much as he did.

Damn it.

Brady entered the house, but Kamden didn't look at him, trapped in a whirlpool of words and revelations. He hadn't meant to hurt Everly, but he had. The knowledge ate at him. He'd told her he was bad for her, hadn't he? He'd told her how he was wired, right?

Yes, he had, but not in a context that mattered.

He never expected to see Delaney again. He didn't know how he'd feel when he set eyes on her again. He'd been as stunned as anyone when he'd unraveled the truth, accepting he was ready to move forward and change his life for the better.

"Give her time," Brady said quietly. "She just needs space."

"I'm not sure about that. You didn't hear what she said or see her face." And then she'd done something he truly hadn't anticipated. "She set Baloo on me too. She said if I didn't back up and leave her alone, she'd turn him loose."

Brady's eyes saucered. "She what?"

"That sweet pony of hers went from adorable to *Cujo* in a heartbeat."

"Do you blame her?" Candice came inside, visibly angry. "What did you expect? You chose another woman in front of her. You didn't talk to her, indicate who she was to you, or ask her opinion on the matter. Do you have any idea how humiliated she felt?"

"Baby," Brady warned, going to her. "He told Delaney to fuck off. He was trying to do the right thing."

Candice looked at Kamden. "Did you tell Everly that?"

How could he? "She wouldn't listen to anything I had to say."

"God, what a cluster." Candice put her hands on her hips. "Tell me everything about Delaney, and then break down how things went with Everly when you walked through that door. I need to hear it all."

Kamden gazed up at her. "Why?"

"Because I'll be there in few days." He met her eyes and noted the compassion and understanding in them. He didn't know if it was because she wanted to make things right, or she felt she had to since Brady was his brother. "I'll talk to her."

Since he had nothing to lose, he did as she said. He started with Delaney, explaining what he'd said, describing how things went down. Then he came to Everly, finding that was harder to talk about. He managed to get through it, giving her the information she wanted. She listened quietly, absorbing it all.

When he finished, she went to the ottoman and sat down. "I didn't get much out of her on the drive here, but I didn't have to. You hurt her, but there's more to it. I'm not sure what since she didn't feel obligated to share."

"What kind of something?"

"It could be anything," Candice offered, peering over at Brady before her attention returned to Kamden. "Something happened to her at some point, I'd wager. Whatever it is, that's why she wanted out of here so quickly. She couldn't handle the emotions going through her. You triggered things, but I don't think you are the only reason she became so aggressive."

"How do you know that?"

"She's been in her shoes," Brady answered for Candice, hurrying over to her, placing his hands on her shoulders. "She knows how it feels."

"We weren't supposed to arrive until Sunday, but we can come earlier," Candice sighed. "The earliest I can get away is Friday. We can drive to your place, and I can talk to her for you. She might not want you around, but she didn't say anything about me."

"You'd do that?" Kamden appreciated her help, but he wanted to know why she'd put her neck out for him.

"I love your brother. He means everything to me," she replied, leaning against Brady. "If you're not happy, he won't be happy. I won't have him hurt if I can help it." Her large blue eyes softened. "I also think you deserve a second chance. Everyone does."

"Maybe it's best if I leave her be." He'd known he was bad for Everly. Awful things seemed to follow him wherever he went. "I don't want to hurt her more than I already have."

"Then don't, idiot," Brady said, his voice a low growl. "Do you what you told me." He peered down, studying Candice. "Love the hell out of her."

Could he do that? Was it possible?

He thought about the time he'd spent with Everly, recalling how she made him feel like a new man. She'd had him thinking of things he'd never thought he would again, of a life spent with someone else. He wanted her by his side, caring for and loving her if she'd let him.

That was the problem.

She didn't want those things from him, not anymore.

There was only one thing to do. If he wanted her, he had to do everything he could to prove himself. He had to give her a reason to trust him again. It might not work, but he'd never know how things could have been if he didn't try.

"If Candice can get through to her," he told Brady, "I'll make sure that happens."

"Oh, I'll get through to her." Candice sounded confident. "But you better think ahead. You think of the things you know about her and get ready to show her why you're worth it. If you don't, you won't have to worry about the pony dog. I'll tear into your ass myself."

Kamden studied the couple in front of him.

He felt the love they had for each other, able to see it in their faces and shared touches. They'd found something special together, something he never thought he'd want for himself. He'd done so much to avoid emotional attachment, believing he was keeping himself safe. What he hadn't known was that by doing so, he'd lost out on so fucking much.

"You'll come Friday?" he asked the pair.

"We will," Candice answered. "I'll talk to her."

He nodded and said, "I need a way home. I only took off for a couple of days. I can't stay away from work all week."

"You can borrow my truck," Brady said. "We're renting an SUV for the trip."

Kamden would have to make it home and bide his time.

Everly warned him about stepping onto her property.

All he could do was wait.

And hope.

CHAPTER TEN

EVERLY TRIED TO focus on work, putting the finishing touches on the fireplace, but found no joy in her efforts. The last few days had been miserable and long. There was a good reason for it, and she had no choice but to accept she'd gone and messed things up.

In fairness, she hadn't realized it until it was too late.

As soon as she'd hit the Alabama state line, she'd reverted to her old self. She cringed when she remembered evoking the one-strike rule, delivering it directly to Kamden with all the venom built up inside her. Her father had chastised her about that, disapproving of the habit. He lectured her about the power of forgiveness, warning her hate didn't do anyone any good. He'd told her the tendency to toss people out of her life was a dangerous thing, warning it would eventually hurt her instead of those she was angry at.

As always, her father had been right.

When she recalled what Kamden had told her without the steady haze of anger and hurt, she'd started to wonder precisely what he'd told Delaney.

What she did brought me to you.

You wouldn't be in my life if she was still a part of it.

Had he meant it? Did it really happen that way?

There was a solid chance she'd never know. She'd made herself clear, showing him how awful she could be if she wanted to. She'd even turned Baloo on him, something that made her feel deeply ashamed. He'd gotten the message right away, knowing she meant it, allowing her to leave. In retrospect, he'd made the smart decision. Then and there, in that dangerous and volatile moment, she wanted to hurt him as much as he'd hurt her.

Embarrassment built when she'd made it home.

She'd lashed out like a spoiled brat.

The next day she'd started reaching out to those who could appraise the house. That was the first step she had to take to put the house and land on the market. She didn't want to leave the area, as she'd established an understanding with the rescue she adored, but she didn't think she could stay. Even now, she found herself going outside numerous times during the day, monitoring the house in the distance, hoping to see Kamden visiting his parents. She'd made sure to take his truck to his place as soon as she could, leaving it with the keys in the ignition as she'd slowly made her way back to her place using crutches and sheer determination.

But she hadn't seen him.

Not once.

Maybe he had lied to her. Perhaps he'd stayed in Tennessee to reunite with his ex. The very idea made her sick. The woman had hurt him the worst way, but she knew people often gravitated toward those they wanted at any cost. She had to stop blaming herself. He'd disregarded her at the table and went with the redhead, after all. Leaving her with people she'd just met.

She jumped when she heard a knock at the door, followed by Baloo's deep barking. Her heart skipped a beat and increased its rhythm. Lowering the brushes in her hand, she told herself it was probably a delivery. She'd ordered numerous things to finish what she'd started, and they were arriving today and tomorrow.

To sell the house, she had to get things in order.

It took longer than she liked to make it to the door. The boot came in handy, keeping her ankle stable, but if she pushed too hard, she'd have to take a break. She'd already pushed her body to its limit. She didn't bother with the peephole, flinging the door open. She started when she saw Candice standing on the porch. She'd dressed for cold, wearing a sweater, jeans, and boots.

What is she doing here? "Candice?"

"It's me." Candice shot her a smile. "Can I come in?"

"Uh, sure." Everly stepped back, giving her room.

"Holy shit." Candice gazed around, taking in the hours of labor and hard work. She stared at the fireplace and the walls, studying the floor and ceiling. "You did all this?"

"I did." Despite the shock, pride surged through her. She worked long and hard to bring this place back from the dead. "You approve?"

"You're going to have to come back to Tennessee. I love Brady's place, but if you could add a little of this, it would really make it home."

The words sent a chill through Everly.

Home. A soft place to fall.

Something she'd never have on her own.

She closed the door. "What are you doing here?"

"Is there somewhere we can talk?" Candice spun around, taking in the living area.

Since the air mattress she'd brought in wouldn't work, there was only one place. "The kitchen." She started in that direction, motioning with her hand, "It's this way."

Baloo followed, and she let him, wanting him next to her. She came to the table and chairs and took a seat, wondering why Candice had decided to pay her a visit.

"Wow." Candice took the kitchen in, too, looking at the counters, coming to the table. "This is amazing."

The kitchen had been her first project. She'd removed the fridge and stove before she'd gotten to work on the cabinets and counters. Since she wanted to maintain the feel of the place, she'd gone with similar colors and patterns. It had taken her over a week to finish things.

"Thank you." She grasped her thermos and poured herself a cup of coffee. "Hopefully, buyers will feel the same way."

That caused Candice to stop admiring things. Her blue eyes shuttered, and she went to the empty chair beside Everly. As she sat, she asked, "You're selling the place?"

She nodded. "I'm hoping to have appraisers come by next week."

"Where will you go?" Candice studied her like she was trying to get a read on her. "What will you do?"

"I'm not sure where I'll go, but there are properties I can flip all over. I've made a file. I just have to choose a project."

"Everly." Candice placed her hand on the table, tapping her fingers against it. "I'm not here to make things harder or tell you what to do. I came to see you because there are things you need to know."

As much as she wanted to hear the things Candice wanted to share, she also didn't. "If it's about Kamden, it might be best if you go." She'd been fighting with herself, wanting to reach out to him as much as she wanted to turn him away. "I can't promise to be nice."

"I'm not afraid of your bad, Everly." Candice met her gaze. "Believe it or not, I have plenty of bad to direct right back at you. You have no idea how much anger I held on to. I've carried it with me for years. If not for Brady, I'd be where I'd always been. Protecting myself, staying away from what I wanted. Sometimes you need help to see what's right in front of you."

She saw the truth in Candice's eyes. In many ways, the heavy emotion in them mirrored her own. "So say it. Get it over with."

"Kamden left the table because he didn't want Delaney anywhere near you. It wasn't because he picked her over you or wanted her. He thought it was beneath you to have to deal with her at all." Candice didn't move, remaining eerily still. "He wanted to begin another chapter in his life, which meant being brutally honest, and he didn't want you anywhere near it when it happened."

"I was there." She tried to remain calm, inhaling through her nose and exhaling through her mouth. "I saw what he did."

"You might have seen, but you don't understand."

Her temper almost broke loose and charged. "Don't I?"

"No, you don't." Candice drew herself up, her gorgeous sapphire eyes no longer sweet but somewhat cold. "Delaney wanted to rekindle things, and he told her no." She inched closer, so her words were clear. "You make him feel things he thought he'd never experience again. He doesn't want her." Candice grasped Everly's hand, using a grip that indicated she wouldn't let go even if Everly tried to pull away. "He wants you."

Everly wanted to believe her but was afraid to. "He doesn't want me. He wants the idea of me."

"You're wrong," the curvaceous blonde stated. "I listened to him. You didn't."

"That's not fair."

"Maybe not," Candice stated, staying in control. "But it's true."

That one-strike rule came to life, telling her to put Candice in her place. Everly forced it back because a part of her wanted—no, that wasn't right, she *needed*—to believe.

"So what did he tell you?" She maintained a hold of herself. "That he was sorry? I've heard that before. Most people don't mean it. They just want to absolve themselves of guilt."

Candice reflected on the question, letting Everly go, trying to find an answer. After several seconds, she decided on what needed to be said, meeting Everly's level glare. "That he's falling for you. He didn't want you near Delaney because he doesn't want you anywhere near his past.

He knows where that'll lead, and he doesn't want to risk it. He's trying to look to the future."

That couldn't be. The Kamden she knew would never admit that.

As soon as that notion came, images of him in the shower arose. He'd taken his time with her, washing her hair, playing with her when she'd decided to start a tickling match. At that moment, he'd become someone else, changing before her eyes.

She reached for Baloo, needing the comfort. "If he wanted to look to the future, he would have told her to piss off. He wouldn't have left me sitting at the table on my own."

"He was wrong to do that," Candice agreed readily. "He knows that now. But try to look at it from his point of view." She lifted her hands, palms up. "He had what he wanted in the one hand and what has held him back in the other. He didn't go about it in the right way, but his intentions were true. He let her go to come back to you."

Tears came, but Everly didn't let them fall. "Why are you telling me this now? I thought you were on my side."

"I'm not taking sides. I'm telling you this now," Candice reached out, stroking a finger across Everly's cheek when a tear managed to escape, "because you're hurting as much as he is. There's no need for it. If you two can stop with the foolishness, this will all be a bad memory."

Everly wanted to lash out, but Candice pulled back. "It's not fair of me to tell you this without telling you my story. I've only shared it with a few people. It doesn't come easy for me, but I know how this feels. You have no idea how hard it'll be to say it out loud. It's the worst feeling in the world. If you're willing to listen, I'll explain my own hurt, so you understand. Once I do, I only ask that you do the same for Kamden."

If it was that difficult, why would she offer it? "Why are you doing this?"

"Because love found me somehow. It came into my life and changed everything. It sounds cheesy, but it's true." Candice watched her, and Everly thought she saw tears in the blonde's eyes. "Will you listen to me now? Or will you turn me away too?"

Seeing the pain in the woman's expression, she nodded. "I'll listen."

Candice settled in, sharing a horrific story that had Everly cringing.

With each word, the wall around her heart shattered and fell. She listened, finding similarities in the tales that were vastly different, taking them into herself. Candice had been hurt horrifically, enduring something Everly didn't think she could have ever gotten over. The blonde cherub had been used in a way that defied imagination, setting her on a path of self-destruction. Brady had found a way to her, breaking through the trauma, showing her that a person was only defined by history if they wanted to be.

By the time Candice finished, Everly wasn't angry.

Not even close.

"He only wants to explain," Candice said quietly. "But that's not up to him. Everything that happens from here on in depends on you."

"He doesn't love me if that's what you think," she stated, believing it. "He loves the idea of me. He thinks I'm the person he built up in his head."

"The same could be said for you too, couldn't it? Brady told me things happened fast between the two of you. The only way you'll find out if this is what you want is if you talk and really get to know each other."

Could she talk to him? Did she want to?

Who are you kidding?

She'd been thinking about him since she'd made it home.

Resigned, accepting the truth, she said, "I'll talk to

him."

"Just decide how you want things to go and take it from there. I would tell you to come over for dinner, but I don't think that's the best place. Brady's parents are great, but they're already talking about a wedding, where we should live, and grandchildren. I'm not sure how my parents will react to that when we have the big family dinner in a month. They still think of me as their baby."

Since Everly didn't spot an engagement ring, she didn't touch the subject. "Sounds complicated."

"Not really, if you don't let it be." Candice reached into her pocket and pulled out a slip of paper. She handed it over, a happy smile on her face. "This is my number. If you ever need to talk, I'll listen."

Everly still didn't get it. Why did Candice want to help her?

"Why are you doing this?" she repeated for what she felt was the billionth time. "Before I talk to him, you have to tell me."

"Someone helped me once. She taught me when you're given a new outlook on life, you pay it forward."

"But you don't know me."

Candice shrugged. "Sabine didn't know me when she reached out. Now she's one of my closest friends."

What more was there to say? The woman seemed to have all her bases covered. Besides, this had to happen. If she didn't talk to Kamden, she'd live to regret it. "I'll meet him tomorrow afternoon. Two o'clock at The Mezzia Luna on the corner of Whitesburg and Jones."

"Does he know where that is?"

"If he doesn't, tell him it's in the shopping center with the pet store. I'm going over in the morning to set up for adoption day."

Candice hesitated. "You don't want to call him your-self?"

"No, not yet. I have to finish the fireplace today. I put

it off for too long. If I get on the phone with him, I'll get off schedule." Hell, it was more than that. *Just be fucking honest.* "I'm not ready to talk to him yet. I have to figure out what I'm going to say."

"Makes sense. I'll tell him." Candice stood and adjusted her sweater. "Just do me a favor. Don't stand him up, all right? I'm trying to make a good impression with the family."

She made it to her feet. "I won't."

Everly walked Candice to the door and went back inside as soon as he saw Brady waiting in a large SUV. She wasn't angry at Kamden's brother, but she wasn't ready to talk to him either.

So Kamden hadn't gone back to his former flame.

The relief that came with the knowledge was profound.

Unfortunately, she was left with a shitton of guilt. If she'd heard him out in the first place, things wouldn't be so messed up.

But Candice mentioned one thing that was certainly true.

Things between her and Kamden had happened extremely fast. Perhaps the best thing to do was to slow things down and get to know each other. Before, they'd went at each other hard and fast, letting their mutual attraction guide them, enjoying mind-blowing sex along the way.

This time around, there had to be more to it.

Things wouldn't last otherwise.

Kamden drove up his driveway, groaning as he stretched his shoulder. He had no problem working with the crew, but with the stress of the last few days, he'd gone overboard. He'd taken his frustrations out on brick, wood, and foundation, wearing himself out. When he got home, he was too exhausted to care about much of anything. Each day he got up early, went to work, and came home worn the fuck out. He had to get a shower and toss back a couple of beers if he wanted to feel anything like himself.

Lights were on in his house, and the SUV Brady had rented was parked out front. Apprehension merged with anticipation. Candice said she'd speak to Everly. If Brady had used his key to get in, she must have driven over at some point during the day. For good or bad, he was about to find out how things went.

He parked the truck, climbed out, and went up the porch. Damn, it had been a long ass day. If God was in a good mood, maybe things were about to turn a corner. He opened the door and was assailed by the delicious aroma of sizzling steak. Brady came from the kitchen with a smile on his face. That boded well. At least, he hoped it did.

"Everly wants you to meet her at Mezzia Luna tomorrow."

"She said that?" A part of him thought she'd tell Candice to go to hell.

Brady nodded. "She did."

Thank fucking God. "What time?"

"Two o'clock."

Worried, he asked, "She's not out for blood?"

"Candice doesn't think so. She's young, Kam. She was hurt and embarrassed. But she's had time to calm down. You just need to slow things down and show her what she means to you. You can't go about things like you were. I know you said you talked and agreed to what was going on between you, but this time around, you need to man up and treat her in a way she deserves. No more of this sneaking around bullshit."

Kamden gazed around. "Shouldn't Candice be telling me this?"

"She's at the hotel. We're leaving a day early."

Damn. "Already?"

Brady looked at the ceiling and groaned. "It's not soon enough. Mom pulled out my photo album. Candice had to sit through all the stories. It was humiliating."

Double damn. "She does like to do that."

"We're heading out in the morning, so she's relaxing while she can, but I wanted to talk to you before we go. I raided your fridge and made something. The food is still warm, but it won't stay that way."

Kamden got a beer, went to the table, and took a seat. He hadn't eaten anything that remotely resembled food in days. As an added bonus, his brother was extremely adept in the kitchen. He studied the plate, and his stomach growled. The steak was rare, just the way he liked it, and the sweet potato beside it had been buttered.

"I haven't told you a lot about Candice and me, just that she was hurt by someone," Brady said, sliding into the chair across from him. "It took a lot of effort on my part to get over that. If you really want to do this right, you're going to have to take a step back and rethink your strategy."

That was something he already knew. "I've been thinking about it this week."

"Are you sure this is what you want?"

"I wouldn't have had your girl talk to her if I wasn't."

"I'm not fucking around, Kam. Is this girl who you want?"

The way Brady said it had Kamden ripping his attention from his food. "What's the matter, Bray?"

"I was worried about Everly, but you're my brother. If it comes down to it, you're the one that matters to me. I don't want her to hurt you."

"Did she indicate that's what she had in mind?" There was a possibility she'd agreed to meet and talk to cut him from her life once and for all. But if that was the case, why do it in public? He'd seen her angry, but he didn't think she was a completely vengeful person. "Is she going to give me a taste of my own medicine?"

"No, nothing like that. It's something else."

Kamden put down his utensils. "Out with it. What aren't you telling me?"

"You're going to have to give her a reason to stay," Brady stated. When Kamden arched a brow in question, Brady dropped the bomb. "She told Candice she's selling the house."

He'd managed to keep a grip on himself, but hearing that had him balling his hands into fists. She was going to meet with him but planned on leaving. Fuck. He retrieved his beer, taking another drink. He was too old for this shit. As much as he wanted her, he hadn't lied when he said he wasn't good at this song and dance. He was a simple man with simple wants and needs. He didn't know how to wine and dine a woman. His romance with Delaney started when he was sixteen. Back then, stupid gestures had gotten him by. Those things wouldn't work now.

"I don't know what in the fuck I'm supposed to do about that."

"Can I make a suggestion?" Brady asked.

It couldn't hurt. "Why not?"

"Don't give her your cock."

Kamden choked on the beer, coughing as he blurted, "What the fuck?"

"If you want to get sexual, keep it at foreplay. Don't give her the real thing until you are on the same page."

"Is this one of the kinky things you like to do?" A few years ago, Kamden had seen Brady sporting a fucking collar of all things. He'd confessed he liked to submit to women on occasion, indicating his sex life wasn't exactly vanilla. Since it wasn't hurting anyone, Kamden had taken the information at face value, deciding his brother was a grown man who could make his own decisions. "I don't think Everly will be into any of that."

"It has nothing to do with kink." Thankfully, his sibling didn't appear offended. "It's about deciding where things will go. You put sex first, and look where it got you."

"So I just come out and tell her 'sorry, darlin'. The cock is off-limits'?"

Brady appeared amused, grinning. "If you want a PG rating, you can tell her you want to take things slow."

"That's probably better." He was already in hot water. No need to kick things up another notch. Curious, he asked, "You really think that'll work?"

"It did with Candice."

Holy hell. "You did that to her?"

"I told her I didn't want a casual relationship. To underscore the point, I gave her something to look forward to when we took things to another level. Anticipation has a way of moving things along. Wind her up, so she's always ready to see you. Keep her wanting more."

"Shit, Bray."

"It's just a suggestion."

Kamden went back to his food. "I'll take it under advisement."

"Can I say something else?"

"Why ask?" His brother was on a roll. "You're going to do it anyway."

"You should work on your appearance. No offense, but you look like shit."

Something he already knew. "It's been a long week."

Brady's gaze went to Kamden's hands. "I can tell."

"It's what I do. She knows that." He couldn't correct the damage by tomorrow. Blisters and cuts took time to heal. "I'll make sure to shower and shave."

"Bring her flowers too."

Enough of this shit. "I might not do romance, but I understand the concept. I'll clean myself up, make myself presentable, and treat her like a lady."

His brother didn't seem convinced, but he dropped it. "Has Delaney called you again?"

"She has, but I haven't answered. I'd still like to know where the fuck she got my number." Apparently, his ex had heard about Everly leaving. Afterward, she'd spoken to someone who handed her his digits. He'd answered once, not recognizing the number, and had ended the call as quickly as possible. "If she keeps it up, I'll have it changed."

"She never liked being told no, but you know that."

That he did. Back in the day, she'd throw a tantrum if she didn't get her way. "I'd forgotten how pushy she can be."

"I never did care for her."

Brady was always cordial and polite to women. Knowing how he felt about Delaney said a lot. "I should have listened to you when I had a chance," Kamden admitted. "I was young and stupid."

"She was your first. That certainly didn't help."

That was a big difference between the brothers. Although he was younger, Brady had had several sexual partners before he turned eighteen. Kamden hadn't had the same experience, falling for the first girl he asked out. That was one of the primary reasons he tried to make things work when they'd drifted apart.

Back then, he couldn't imagine life without her.

Brady decided to shut up and eat, so Kamden did the same. He did have some planning to do. Maybe Brady was right. The sexual aspect of things wasn't the problem. He and Everly had to tackle something bigger. They had to learn to trust each other. He wasn't sure how to go about it, but he hoped Everly was on the same page. He wouldn't know until he talked to her openly for the first time.

Tomorrow was going to be a big day.

CHAPTER ELEVEN

EVERLY FIDGETED IN her seat, her eyes darting from the table to the door. She glanced at her watch, noting it was ten minutes until two. Was Kamden going to show? Maybe he decided she wasn't worth the effort. She'd laid into him like he was the worst man alive. If he chose not to speak to her, she'd have to accept it.

I only have myself to blame.

She ran her fingers through her hair, hoping she'd upped her game a little. Before she'd come to the restaurant, she'd used the bathroom at the pet store. She'd changed into more appealing clothing, taking time with her hair and makeup. Since time was short, she had to rush. Hopefully, if he decided to show up, he'd like what he saw.

The door opened, and she held her breath. When she saw who entered, she immediately ducked her head. What were the fricking odds? She'd seen Brett at the adoption event but had managed to shake him. He really needed to move on and find someone else. She hadn't expected him to visit the restaurant. She chanced a peek, looking to see where the hostess sat him, and saw him heading in her direction.

"Everly, hey," he said, stopping at the table. "Can I join you?"

She didn't want to be rude, but she'd had about enough. "I'm meeting someone, actually."

"Can I wait with you?" He gave her a boyish smile.

Shit.

Before she could answer, the door opened again.

Kamden stepped inside.

She wanted Brett away from the table. Immediately.

"He's here now," she said, trying to be polite.

Brett didn't move away, and Kamden came on over. She took measured breaths, unsure of how things would go. She cursed her choice of venue, thinking it would have been better if she'd met Kamden somewhere away from the adoption event. Then Brett wouldn't have been anywhere nearby.

Kamden handed her a bouquet of roses and glanced at Brett. "Small world."

"I was at the adoption event." Brett had never been rude, but she could see he wasn't happy about the interruption. "How about yourself?"

"My motives are purely selfish." Kamden gazed at her, meeting her eyes. He didn't look angry, but he didn't look pleased. "I'm here for her."

Brett studied her for a moment. "Then I'll leave you to it."

She didn't realize she'd been holding her breath until he walked away.

"I told you," Kamden said, sliding into a chair. "He's determined."

To hell with Brett. The man she wanted to see was finally here. He'd shaved and—while his bristle-free face was sublime—she discovered she preferred him with a bit of stubble. He dressed as he usually did, but he'd chosen a shirt that appeared new and jeans that weren't faded. When her eyes landed on his forearms and hands, she gasped. There were numerous bruises, blisters, scrapes and cuts.

"What got hold of you?" She'd taken the liberty of ordering him a dark lager. Hoping he'd like that, she passed it over. "Doesn't that hurt?"

"It's fine. Don't worry about it." He glanced at the beer. "You ordered this for me?"

"I hope you don't mind."

"Not at all." He took a healthy drink, licking his lips. "It's good."

"So, uh..." Where did she start? What the hell did she say?

He smiled, and suddenly, the tension between them faded. "This is awkward, right?"

"Extremely."

"I'll go first." He took another drink, put the glass down, and met her gaze. "I handled things badly, but I don't regret what I told Delaney. You shouldn't be anywhere near my ex, because you're too good for her. I told her I'd moved on, and it was over." He pulled his phone from his pocket and placed it on the table. "So everything is in the open. She's been calling me. I don't know how she got my number. I have no interest in her and will tell her to fuck off if she calls again."

"No," she responded right away, glaring at the phone. She lifted her eyes and looked at him. "You might not want me around her, but if she calls again, you hand the phone to me. I want to be the one to tell her to fuck off."

"Easy enough." He pushed the phone toward her. "I listed her contact as Bitch. Have at it."

Just like that, she relaxed and felt a smile tugging at her lips. "Did you really?"

"If you don't believe me, take a look."

She accepted the challenge, taking the phone. She swiped the screen, opened the list that contained his contacts, and found what she was looking for. The picture for the number was Darth Vader. Holy shit. When he hated, he hated all the way.

Shocked and surprised, she questioned, "That's really why you did it? You didn't want her around me?"

"I don't want her breathing the same air you do, darlin'."

Well hell. "I shouldn't have acted like a spoiled brat. You weren't the only one who acted badly."

"You're going to have to tell me what that was about. I might have pissed you off, but it wasn't all about me."

That was something she already knew. "It was the one-strike rule."

"Want to define that for me?"

It was only fair he knew. "I started it after my mother. One strike and a person is out. It's immature and stupid, I know."

"Just don't use it on me again," he warned, his amber-hued eyes narrowing. "If you've got a problem, you talk to me about it. It wasn't fair to use Baloo like that, by the way. I really thought you were going to send him over the couch."

"I know." Shame rolled through her and her cheeks heated. She studied the phone in her hand, fiddling with it. "I'm sorry. I was angry and felt trapped. I just wanted to get out and go home."

"So long as we're in agreement. You talk to me if something's wrong, and I'll do the same. No one else needs to be drawn into the middle of our arguments. Both of us went about things in the wrong way. Let's not do it again, all right?"

The waitress came to the table, and they both got the lunch special. She didn't think she could eat as her stomach was off-kilter, but at least she'd have something to move around on a plate.

"So what now?" she questioned, afraid to look at him.

"Now we talk about what we're expecting out of this. Before, it was to give each other a chance. I didn't clarify what I wanted, other than all your free time. I think it's best to get that out of the way because if what we want is different, we're wasting our time. Don't you agree?" When she nodded, he went first. "I don't want casual with you. I'm putting that out there right now. If, for whatever reason, things don't work, I'll respect that. But that's what I'm after. I'm going to tell people I'm involved with someone, and I expect you to do the same."

That shocked her because he avoided that very thing. "That's really what you want?"

"It's absolutely what I want," he answered. "How about yourself?"

He was offering her what she'd wanted from the start. "The same."

"The same?" he asked, tilting his head.

"I want the same thing you do." He'd been honest with her. It was time to give as good as she'd gotten. "I don't want to hide what we are to each other. I want us to be a couple."

"I also think we should slow things down." Her confusion must have been noticeable because he clarified, "We hit the ground running with things if you catch my drift. This time we're going to appreciate each other in a different way."

He wasn't saying what she thought he was. "Are you saying we won't have sex?"

"That's exactly what I'm saying." He picked up the beer, nursing it slowly.

She couldn't say she liked that.

What the hell have I done?

He couldn't believe it. Brady's advice worked, after all.

Even now, he could see her displeasure, the way her spine straightened as she shifted in her seat. That was too bad because he'd had time to think things over and decided his brother was right. They already knew they were compatible between the sheets. To take things further, they had to decrease the heat and enjoy each other in other ways.

Now it was time to lay out his plan. "I'm going to alternate between work and helping you with your place. I'm not sure how I'll rotate it, but you can expect to see a lot of me. That'll give us a chance to be around each other, talk, and spend time together. You're welcome to visit my place, so long as you know it won't be like last time."

"You're going to help me with my house?"

"I am." It was a dangerous move, as the work would be done faster, and she could choose to leave once it was completed. He had to show her she could count on him and trust him. "I can take care of the barn, trees, and things on the outside."

"I'm supposed to help with adoption events this month." Since she hadn't anticipated him being around, she'd agreed right away when asked. "Saturdays mornings will be booked for me."

"I can come with you or meet you when you get home."

Now she was completely taken off guard. "You'd come to the events?"

"I already told you." He put his glass down and reached for her hand. As soon as he had it, he informed her, "I'm not hiding what's going on. If we're going to be together, we're really going to be together. Just know if I come, I'll tell people you're mine. Your friend Brett is in for a rude awakening." Some people would notice the age difference, but he no longer gave a flying shit. "You'd better be ready for that."

"If you're willing to come to the events, I want you there. It'll be another couple of weeks before I can really move around, so you'd be a big help." She frowned, releasing his hand, flipping it over. He had open blisters on a couple of fingers and his palm. She drew a breath through her teeth, hissing at what she saw. "Jesus, what did you do?"

"Work without gloves." Technically, he'd also moved things with sharp edges he should have avoided. "Don't worry, Mom. I'll make sure to use them this week."

Her hazel eyes lifted, and she crinkled her nose. "Ass."

"I've been called it a time or two."

She cautiously touched the wounds. "Doesn't it hurt?"

"It did." The way he spoke had her peering up. Their eyes met, and he told her, "Somehow, you're making it all better."

Her lips twitched, the corners curving. "Now you're a sweet talker."

"Which do you prefer?"

"Both."

Their food came, forcing them to break apart. She didn't like it, and neither did he, but they both eased back. He'd never been to the place before, so he'd followed her lead. The dish looked appetizing, even if the portions were smaller than hell.

With some things out of the way, they had to address the elephant in the room.

It was time to find out how she wanted to deal with it.

"We're going to have to tell my parents about us. They'll eventually notice me at your place and ask about it." He watched as he said it, studying her face and body language. She froze, her hands going still. "I don't mind doing it right away if that's what you want, but they can be nosey and pushy. I can tell them to give you space and leave you alone, but they'll be inviting you over for every single dinner, holiday, and every other thing in between."

"That bothers you?"

"No, because I've made up my mind. I'm telling you because it might bother you. They mean well, but the attention might feel suffocating. Especially since they already like you."

"That can't be that different from how they treat me now."

She was about to find out how wrong she was. "You say that now, but you'll see. Candice and Brady decided to leave a day early because of it."

"What?" Concern and worry shone through her eyes. "It's that bad?"

"Not bad, per se. Just intrusive. Candice is Brady's first real relationship, so they went at them pretty hard. I had a taste of things, but that was a long time ago. Our parents want to see us settled." They'd started in on the brothers when Kamden turned thirty, worried their sons would never find the right person for them. "They've been harping on us for years."

"What are the rules when it comes to them?"

He didn't understand the question. "How do you mean?"

"Will you get pissed if I tell them to mind their own business?"

She'd do it, too. He knew how ballsy she was. "I don't want you using your one-strike rule. They don't mean any harm. If possible, you have to be polite."

"I want to be open about things, but I don't want to piss them off if I don't have to." She took a deep breath and asked, "Do you mind if we wait until they ask questions?"

"Not at all, but I needed to know." She didn't like talking about her family, but he also wanted to know how that part of things would go. "What about you? Any family I need to know about?"

When she didn't speak for several seconds, he wondered if she would at all. "Just an aunt and uncle. We don't speak often. I send them a Christmas card each year." She wriggled in her seat, moving the food around on her plate. "My mother reaches out here and there. I have a half-sister, but we've never met or spoken to each other."

He sat up, surprised to hear it. "Why not?"

"I'm not ready to meet her." She looked around the room, avoiding his gaze. "I found out about her when I was little. I didn't want to hear about her. As I got older, I thought about talking to her, but I didn't think things would go well. We've had very different upbringings. We'll probably end up arguing."

"Does that bother you?" It seemed like it did. It sure as shit would bother him.

"Sometimes," she admitted, shrugging. "She's a part of me I may or may not know. I'm still undecided about all of it. She graduates this year."

"I'm about to ask an extremely personal question. I won't be mad if you choose not to answer it." He waited for her to give him the go-ahead before he asked, "Why did your mother leave your father?"

"He wasn't rich or exciting enough." The answer was so soft, he had to strain to hear it. She cleared her throat and met his eyes. "The only times Daddy liked to go out was when he was hunting, fishing, or working. That wasn't enough for her. She wanted to travel the world and went looking for the man that could give that to her. When she found him, she left."

"Both of you?"

"She visited here and there, sending me presents from different places, but yeah, for the most part. She didn't express any real interest until she got pregnant with my sister. That's when she tried to come back into my life. She wanted us to be close, but I wouldn't let it happen. By then, the damage was done."

"Have you ever asked her why?"

He saw the anger in her then, the disgust. "I don't care why. I was raised by one parent and one parent only. Dad was there in the good times and the bad. He's the one that loved and raised me, not her. She might have given me life, but she isn't my mother."

Damn. Not good. "I'm guessing that's changed your perspective on things."

The fury in her eyes dimmed. "How do you mean?"

"About having a family of your own."

"When I get married and have children, I will love their father, and he'll love me. There won't be separations or divorces. I won't settle for anything less. No child should go through what I did. It's not fair, and it's not right."

"I guess I'd better up my game," he told her, teasing somewhat, wanting to see how she'd respond.

"Unless you plan on going out every weekend, partying, or asking me to go on trips to other parts of the world, you're fine." She raked a hand through her hair, and he noted her trembling. "I'm happy where I am. I don't have to venture to new places to carve out my place in the world. The ground I'm currently standing on has always been good enough as far as I'm concerned. I'm content with who I am and what I have."

He believed that since he'd seen how little she left her house. She appeared to be a homebody like him, perfectly happy to come home after a long day. "You don't have to worry about that with me. If I have to go somewhere, I do it on wheels." Seeing her curiosity, he told her the absolute truth, "I don't like planes."

She arched one of her brushstroke brows. "Afraid of flying?" He nodded, and she informed him, "Statistically speaking, planes are safer than cars."

"Sure they are." He played along, wanting to ease the strain in her face. "Unless you have engine trouble. Then statistics go right out the window. Literally."

"I've only been on a few flights myself, and I can't say I loved them."

Interesting. "To where?"

When she smiled, he knew she was reflecting on a happy memory. "My dad worked on a house in Maine once. It was nice there. I loved the water and view. When

I got older, he took me to Disney World. It was beautiful as I thought it would be. We spent four days there."

"Really? I've never been."

"That's a shame."

Her grin had his entire body tingling. Despite his decision to keep things non-sexual, his dick had a mind of its own, jerking as it came to life and hardened.

"Really," he questioned, liking her this way. "Why?"

"All the good attractions are gone or on the way out. You missed the good stuff."

"Well, darlin'," he purred, grinning right back at her, "I have you to tell me about what I missed, don't I?" She blushed again, and fuck if the color didn't suit her. "So I know about your Saturday plans, but I need to know the rest. What does your day look like tomorrow? Any plans?"

She shook her head. "Not really. I planned to work on the bedrooms. The floors are fine, but the closets and walls are a mess. I'm going to have to patch them up and get them painted."

"Sounds like fun."

She snorted. "You haven't seen them yet."

"What time should I be there?"

"You mean it, don't you?" she questioned, full of wonder, like she never believed such a thing would be possible. "You're going to help me with the house."

He shifted his plate out of the way and grasped her hand. "Everything I've said to you, I mean." Seeing the light in her eyes had his body responding and his cock saluting her, but he wouldn't give in to it. He was going to do this properly and see where things went. "We're going to take this nice and slow. I'm looking forward to getting to know you, Everly."

Their eyes met again, and there was zero hesitation or restraint.

She gave his hand a squeeze, cautious since she'd seen

their shredded condition. "How does seven sound? I'm finished with the kitchen. I can make breakfast."

That sounded like heaven. He returned the squeeze, waiting to see what tomorrow would bring, and told her, "I'll be there bright and early." He lifted her hand, brought it to his mouth for a kiss, and met her gaze. "Seven it is."

CHAPTER TWELVE

*H*E'S DRIVING ME *crazy.*

Everly tried to focus, taking donations at her table as the event closed down. While she needed to pay attention to people who wanted to help the rescue, she couldn't stop staring at the man strolling around with jeans that hugged his perfect ass and muscular thighs.

For the last two weeks, he'd done just as he promised, helping her with her house. When they wrapped up for the day, he stuck around to spend time with her. He settled with her on the air mattress she used as a bed in the living room, asking her questions and giving her answers, making good on his promise at the restaurant. They'd gotten to know each other, and she wasn't complaining. She knew him in ways that melted her insides and heart. She never wanted to let him go.

But he'd meant what he said.

He wouldn't touch her, not in an intimate fashion.

He kept things nice, tidy, and completely strict when it came to those kinds of things. The best she got was lingering touches and chaste kisses that drove her completely insane. Even when she'd tried to take things further, trying to seduce him, he'd turned her away with a smug grin and a laugh.

If he didn't give her relief soon, she'd lose her mind.

He finished loading up the last kennel, petted the animals through the bars, and came to her. He'd caught on quick, maneuvering through things, doing the tasks that needed doing. He also informed people he was with her, making it clear they were in a relationship. He brought her water and coffee, smoothed his hand over her head, and placed kisses on her forehead or shoulder. A few women had come on to him, but he'd shaken his head, looked at her, and told them why he was there. He referred to her as *my girl* when people questioned him, making everything perfectly clear. It was apparent who he was in her life, and she couldn't be happier about it.

He was absolute in his resolve.

There was only one thing she wanted and needed.

If only he would give it to her.

Please, God. Give me strength.

Her boot would come off next week, so she could do the things he'd been taking care of on adoption day. She wondered if he'd come back and join her, feeling fairly certain he would. He was fantastic with the cats and canines up for adoption, able to settle them in a way that made her appreciate him all the more. He could soothe each with a touch or softly spoken words, calming the animals like it was second nature.

Just like he does with me.

She glanced up, watching Brett wandering over to Kamden, stopping his progress when they came face-to-face. The men spoke casually, completely at ease with each other, having a discussion she couldn't make out. As much as the veterinarian seemed to like her, she thought he liked Kamden even more.

How could he not?

Kamden was everything a person should be.

Helpful. Polite. Resourceful.

The men had spoken to each other at the first event, coming to terms with each other, uniting for a common cause. After their first discussion, they got along swimmingly. They often spoke, joking with each other, forming what she believed was a strong camaraderie.

Somehow the two actually became friends. It shouldn't have been possible but, then again, who was she to judge that kind of thing?

Kamden laughed, nodded at Brett, and resumed his trek.

He met her gaze and winked, causing her sex to clench.

She wasn't sure how, but she had to end the sexual frustration.

The first week she'd used her vibrator, achieving mild but paltry relief, trying to tell herself it was more than enough. As time passed, she found artificial devices scratched the itch but didn't give her what she really wanted. Each time she smelled Kamden and took him in, she wanted more, fully comprehending she needed him to be as he'd been before. She wanted him to whisper dirty things as he took her however he wanted.

Upon the realization, she'd asked if they could spend the night together, hoping she could tease him into submission. He'd shaken his head, not wanting to give her that, until she'd had enough and pressed the issue. He'd finally relented, bringing clothing to her place to shower and change for work, even though he warned there wouldn't be any sex involved.

It felt like she'd won a major battle in the war.

She'd cooked for him, cared for him, and tried to take things further. Still, he hadn't crossed the line, holding her while she slept, keeping her close but refusing to touch her sexually.

They were both eager for what could happen between them. Even if he denied it, she'd felt his response to her nearness.

And she was tired of waiting.

No matter what he said, she could feel what she did to him.

A voice inside her head told her he knew that as well.

He approached, his focus entirely on her, and moved

like a sly panther on the prowl as he weaved through the people in his path. She watched him as he closed the distance, hoping he'd finally relent and give her what she wanted.

He made it to her side, coming so close she wanted to scream.

He nuzzled her neck and whispered, "It's time to go. Are you ready?"

Am I ever. "I'm ready."

She'd ditched the crutches days ago, as she no longer needed them. She rose from the chair she'd been placed in, eager to see what he had in store. He took her arm, making sure she was balanced, ready to catch her if she fell as he took her to his truck. As soon as she was in the passenger seat, he closed the door and came around, waving to people who called out to him as they departed.

Once inside, he put the keys in the ignition and looked at her. "Brett finally asked Allison out. He wants to know if we want to double."

Allison had tried to get Brett's attention for months. While she was happy for them, she was also cranky. Brett would get his while she was waiting for hers.

That wasn't fair.

"Do you want to?" she asked, aware she sounded like a brat.

"It's up to you. I told him I had to ask first."

"If you want to, we can," she said, studying his profile, thinking it was wrong that one single man had such sex appeal. "Whose place? Mine or yours?"

It was a double entendre, proposed to tell him she wanted to change things. She hadn't been to his house since the first time. At first, she'd wondered why, thinking he had something up his sleeve. As time had gone by, she realized he was saving his place for the big night. When he took her there, they'd cave to the desire between them.

"You naughty, naughty girl," he finally replied with a

laugh. He shot her a wink, his whiskey-colored eyes teasing. "It's only been two weeks."

"Tomorrow starts the third week officially." She'd counted the days, so she knew. He'd kept her riding the edge for too long. If something didn't give, she'd break. "If that's what it takes, invite them over."

He backed up and pulled out of the parking lot. She didn't push, knowing he'd make his own decision. He'd warned her how things would be, and he'd stuck to it. A part of her was tempted to pout. She wanted more from him, but they'd agreed to things early on. He wanted to do this right, and he'd made that evident. As much as she respected his decision, the pent-up frustration was driving her wild.

When she didn't say anything, he said softly, "You can come to my place tonight if you want, darlin'. We won't have sex, but we can play a little."

The word *play* had her shivering in anticipation. "What kind of play?"

"The kind that'll turn that frown of yours upside down."

A flush crept over her, and she thought it was too good to be true. "Don't tease me," she warned, knowing if he did, she'd lose what little control she held over herself. "I've abided by the rules, but I'm at my wits' end. You're driving me nuts, Kamden."

He took in the words, studying the road. "I'm not teasing you, Everly." He reached over, took her hand, and placed it over his crotch. "Do you feel that, baby?"

She certainly did, and it made her hotter and wetter.

He was fully engorged, his erection long and thick.

"What do you have in mind?" Tossing his own words back at him, she murmured, "Can you define play for me?"

"We'll enjoy each other without my cock coming anywhere near your pussy," he answered, observing the road.

As moisture coated her underwear, her desire ramping up, he grinned. "I bought something for you, baby. It came this week."

Oh dear God. "What kind of something?"

"Something you'll like."

He didn't have to ask again. She wanted to go to his place. "What about—"

In an instant, he shushed her. "We'll get Baloo first. Don't worry."

Aching and frustrated, she complained, "Why are we still waiting?"

"I think we feel the same way about each other now," he answered, keeping her palm on the firm length of his cock, moving her hand so she stroked the entire span of it, shifting his hips up and down. "We've had time to talk and understand each other. What comes after will be more than that. We won't fuck tonight because we'll have something to look forward to tomorrow. I wanted to make sure you understand how things will go."

"I can't take much more of this," she confessed, wriggling in the seat, hating the panties that rubbed against parts of her but wouldn't get the job done. "If you're trying to torment me, it's working."

"That's not what I'm doing, baby." He moved her hand, placing it on the center partition, threading his fingers through hers. "I'm only letting you know I've had you on my mind, even if you didn't know it." He glanced at her, and her breath caught when she met his gaze. "If you want, I'll take you home tonight. I can't promise you'll like what I'm going to do to you, but I'm pretty sure you will."

"Do you mean it? About tomorrow?" She really fucking hoped so.

"I sure do."

"Then we'll do things your way." If he wanted her at his place, he had to grant a concession. She hoped he wouldn't turn the offer down. "But I want something in return."

"What's that, baby?"

Never one to talk dirty, she had to force the words from her mouth. "Can I at least suck your cock?"

While he didn't let her go, she noticed his profile change. She'd managed to shock him.

She felt him squeeze her hand, his grip almost painful. "Is that something you want?"

"Are you serious? I've wanted it for weeks." The man had to know that.

He took it in, driving them home. "I'm won't say no if you decide you want that, if that's what you're asking. But tonight is all about you, sweetness."

"Then get Baloo and take me to your place." She didn't hesitate, wanting to unlatch her seat belt, climb over the barrier between them, and take him between her lips now. Even if he didn't get her off, she wanted that one small thing. She hadn't appreciated the blowjob she'd given him before, unaware the mere thought of a repeat would drive her so crazy now. "I want to be with you in that way if you'll let me," she confessed, studying his face. "I'll take whatever you're offering. Just give me that."

"Are you sure?"

I'm more than that. "Pretty please."

He glanced at her, lips curving into a sinful grin. "Your very wish is my command, darlin."

Thank you, Brady. I owe you.

His brother was a fucking saint.

At first, he thought the idea of withholding his cock was sadistic. What kind of man did that to a woman? Keeping her constantly aroused without relief? Turning her on even if he didn't plan on getting her off?

Then he'd gotten jive to the advice, taking it as gospel.

149

It had more than worked.

By denying Everly his cock, he'd gotten to know the young woman he wanted on an entirely new level. They could tease and flirt, constantly picking on each other, playing silly games that had them rolling with laughter but didn't lead to sex. In many ways, it reminded him of his youth. He could be like this with her, allowing her to see a side of him he'd kept tucked away. She'd responded to it, reaching into his soul, draining away the poison of his past. The last two weeks had been amazing, giving him time to understand the gorgeous woman.

She had a heart as vast as the ocean, determined to help people and the animals she loved, wanting to make a difference. They'd spent time together as they'd worked on her house and at the rescue, actually talking for the first time. Although he'd been wary of doing adoption events with her, he'd found his groove right away. He'd gotten to know the people she called friends, finding they were good people.

As they'd opened up to him, he'd uncovered part of himself.

Doing things for the animals under the rescue's care had opened a door in his heart, allowing him to fully understand the woman he wanted to make his. So many of the animals under their care needed love and assistance, all of which she readily offered. Since she'd brought that aspect of things into his life, he accepted he liked to provide it as well.

He'd been concerned when he'd learned about her mother and sibling, thinking she'd closed off part of her heart from everyone, including him. In a couple of weeks, he'd learned she saved that part of herself for creatures that wouldn't judge her. When he'd accepted that, seeing it firsthand, it wasn't easy to keep his hands to himself. He wanted to be with her night and day, watching as she grinned, listening as she laughed.

Everly Mason was sheer fucking perfection.

God Almighty.

He wanted her like hell on fire.

It hadn't been easy to leave her side when she'd asked him to stay. He'd wanted to take her in so many ways, but he'd denied himself, trying to give both of them time, doing the right thing even when he went to bed with a rock-hard dick that kept him awake at night.

She hadn't let up either, asking for the same thing each day.

He'd eventually agreed to sleep over but nothing more. In doing so, he'd only tormented himself. Feeling the curve of her ass against his engorged dick, knowing she was wet and eager for him, made it impossible to think about anything other than fucking her. He knew that would come soon enough when he told her how he felt about her. If he was lucky, she'd reciprocate the sentiment.

He loved the adorable woman and didn't want to live without her.

When she'd asked if she could suck his cock, he thought he'd come then and there. He felt a pulse from the tip, the thick pre-come staining and marking his underwear and jeans.

He wondered if she knew precisely what she was asking for.

If she did take him in her mouth, he'd come hard.

He didn't think either of them could handle much more.

When he pulled up to her house, his voice was hoarse and raspy. "I've already packed a bag." When her head whipped around and she looked at him, he couldn't prevent the shit-eating grin on his face. He'd packed ahead, knowing this day would come. "I have things ready, baby. I'll get Baloo and bring him to the truck."

He opened his door and used the key she'd given him

to go inside. Baloo came to him, wagging his tail, and he patted his head as he went to the attic that had brought them together in the first place. He'd packed a bag for her early on, hoping she wouldn't notice the things he'd taken from the dryer one at a time.

Once he had it, he cautiously made his way down, not wanting to put a damper in things by busting his own ass, and hiked the stairs back up. He didn't bother with Baloo's food or dishes, having ordered both when he'd made up his mind to bring Everly home. The dog's things had arrived with a few other items a couple of days ago, making the evening possible.

"Come on, boy," he said, a bounce in his step, ready to go.

The dog barked, and he wondered if the animal sensed his mood.

He'd waited long enough.

Tonight he'd give Everly what she wanted.

As he locked the door, turned to the truck, and saw her face through the windshield, he accepted she was the one for him. No other would ever do. No woman even came close.

Her simply posed question came back to him.

Can I at least suck your cock?

Hell yes, she could.

But first, he'd show her that she meant everything to him.

CHAPTER THIRTEEN

EVERLY FINISHED MAKING dinner, trying not to think about her libido, and went through the same motions she did at her own home. Kamden had been surprised when she'd shown him her skills in the kitchen, telling her she created dishes that tasted better than anything he'd ever eaten. She'd learned to cook numerous things as she'd moved from place to place with her father, finding different spices and recipes along the way. Since Kamden had done the shopping for her, he'd known what to buy for his residence. The fridge was stocked with numerous things to cook and prepare, ranging from fish to steak.

It was like he'd planned everything ahead of time.

She glanced outside the window, noting the sun had almost set, watching him with Baloo. This was something else he did at her place, playing fetch with the enthusiastic canine. Despite what she'd done, ordering her four-legged companion to growl at him to keep him away from her, Kamden didn't seem afraid of the dog. In fact, she knew if she attempted to issue the order again, the animal would give her a baffled look and wouldn't do squat. Once the Greater Swiss Mountain Dog made a friend, he was loyal and obedient.

There was more to it, of course.

The canine adored Kamden. She felt the same way.

Somewhere down the line, she'd fallen in love with him.

She hadn't told him yet, worried it might change things between them. She felt happier than she had in years, and she didn't want to leave anything to chance. How would he react if he heard the words? Would it take him back to horrid memories? Would he revert to his former self? Acting like he didn't need anyone or anything?

She'd definitely liked him before when he'd been dirty and raunchy, but she'd fallen for the man who laughed easily, cared for her, and greeted her with a smile when he came home from work.

She set the table and went to the sliding back door, clearing her throat, getting ready to call for him. He'd left the back entrance cracked so she could tell him dinner was finished. She yelled his name and hurried to get to her seat, wanting to absorb him as he came inside. Since he'd been outside with Baloo jumping all over him, he'd have a fine sheen of sweat and dust on him. The weather had finally turned warm, snow and ice no longer on the ground. He looked best when his hair was mussed and his clothing was slightly dirty.

He slid through the glass doors, making sure Baloo could follow behind him with ease. He shook himself off, sliding his fingers through his hair. The T-shirt was tight, showing off his muscles and chest. He'd also left some stubble on his face since he knew she liked it when he did. With his messy hair and dark eyes, it was going to be hell to keep herself in check.

"What's on the menu?" he asked. "Something smells amazing."

"Mahi Mahi with artichokes and sun-dried tomatoes."

He gazed at her, giving her a wide grin. "I'm a lucky fucking man. You treat me better than I deserve."

He was wrong.

Kamden deserved everything she had and more. "I hope you like it."

"I know I will," he said, walking to the chair next to

hers. "You work magic on everything you touch."

He slid into his seat and grasped the beer she'd put beside the dish. His Adonis features were stunning, putting all other men to shame. He took a deep swig of the lager, and she watched his throat as he swallowed. She imagined herself at his knees, fully aware she'd be drinking him down at some point in the evening.

She'd meant what she said.

She wanted to suckle his cock, eager to reveal how much she'd yearned for it. She studied him as he settled in, hoping she'd gotten things right. The longstanding rumor was food was a way to a man's heart. So far, he seemed to enjoy what she'd placed in front of him. He took the first bite, and she held her breath as she usually did, hoping he'd praise her efforts.

"That's delicious, baby." He flipped the fork around, licking off the sauce, and pulled the fork between his luscious lips as he groaned. "You are an angel in the kitchen."

He had no idea what the visual did to her, making her wet as the ocean. As a pool built between her thighs, she attempted to keep things together, taking a bite of the food. Even doing so, she monitored him, paying close attention. The man got under her skin, creating a constant sexual want and need.

Yes, she loved him. She never wanted to let him go.

But she wanted something else.

Something only he could give to her.

"Do you want to watch a movie?" He kept eating but glanced at her. "We can take advantage of the satellite."

"The laptop wasn't *that* bad," she grumbled.

He'd found her primary device for watching shows, checking the news, and other such things humorous. They'd watched a couple of movies on the small computer. However, doing so hadn't been exciting or all that comfortable since it needed to be close for them to see and hear it. She'd held off on getting internet and cable at the house, deciding she'd finish things before she made the decision to put it on the market or keep it.

They had to talk about that too.

It wasn't fair to keep it from him.

"It is when you compare it to my flat screen," he replied smoothly.

"All right, snob. Since my electronic devices are too cheap, we'll give yours a try." Maybe if they watched a movie, she could interest him in some heavy petting. He said no sex but kissing and touching didn't count, and he did indicate tonight was about her. "I picked the last one, so it's your turn."

His grin created butterflies in her stomach. "I think it's time we watched a horror movie. What do you think?"

"Why? You afraid to watch one by yourself?" She returned his grin, liking it when they engaged in playful banter. They both liked teasing each other. "You need me to protect you?"

"I don't know." He took another bite of his dinner. "Do you think you can?"

"I'll tell you what." She glanced around, pretending to look at exit strategies, then stared at him. "If the shit hits the fan, you run for the door and go for help. Me and Baloo will buy you time."

"You think I'd leave you to face the fire on your own?" He arched a brow, gave her an offended look, and snorted. "Not likely."

"Oh yeah?" She leaned back in the chair, letting her gaze drift up and down his sublime form. "And just what you would do?"

"If someone messed with you?" She nodded, and he answered, "I'd put the beat down on some poor fucker."

She could picture him doing just that. "You'd fight someone for me?"

"In a heartbeat, baby."

My very own Tarzan. "You're such a caveman."

He winked at her, his golden eyes shining. "And you love that about me."

"You're right. I do."

He took his time eating, something she appreciated about him. Although he could be rough around the edges, he had excellent table manners. She finished before him and took her dish and utensils to the sink. The one thing she loved about his place was the dishwasher. The sucker didn't require a heavy rinse beforehand and made everything so much easier. If she kept the house, she was installing one in her kitchen.

Speaking of which.

"Your dad was outside when we drove over. We're going to have to come clean with your parents soon."

They'd noticed him visiting her and had to know he'd been having sleepovers at her place. She'd expected one or both of them to come over, but thankfully that had happened yet. She didn't particularly want it to go down that way either.

Neither of them had anything to hide.

He brought his plate over and started rinsing it off. He seemed relaxed and calm—a very good sign. "Dad called a few days ago. He knows I've been staying with you. I didn't go into details, but I told him we're spending time together and figuring things out. He's not as bad as Mom, and he's definitely not as pushy. He said he'll keep things under wraps for as long as he can, but she's about to start work on her garden."

Meaning she'd be outside and would finally notice.

"We'll face them next weekend at Sunday dinner." That would give them a week to decide how they wanted to go about it. "If that's what you want."

He put his dish and utensils into the washer and came to her. His arm felt firm and strong when he looped it around her waist. She leaned against him, eyes shuttering. God, he smelled good, a mixture of cologne and clean sweat. When they stood like this, she felt protected and cared for. He had the most amazing body and softest touch.

"What I want," he said, rubbing his chin against her shoulder, "is you."

Before she could bask in the feeling, he turned her around and tossed her over his shoulder. She squealed, kicking her legs, aware he wouldn't drop her. His hand landed on her ass with a hard thwack, making her jump.

"Settle down there, darlin'. I got you."

He carried her to the couch and lowered her, easing her onto the leather. When he followed, easing his weight against her, nipping at her neck, she closed her eyes.

Lord above, she'd waited so long for this.

"You want the movie first?" he asked, breezing his lips over her throat. "Or are you in the mood for something else?"

"Screw the movie." She wrapped her legs around his hips, placing her arms around his back. "I'm definitely in the mood for something else."

"Yes, ma'am."

Their lips met, and the contact sent a tremor through her.

When his tongue lashed out, she met it with her own.

They nibbled, sucked, and the kiss became frantic. Her nipples hardened, her clit pulsing. She pulled his T-shirt up, sliding her hands under the soft cotton, stroking his back. The muscles beneath her hands coiled and flexed, and he bucked his hips against hers. She felt the firm length of him, the rigid erection hard and straining. He reached for the hem of her sweater, and she helped him pull the garment up her torso and over her head.

His mouth caressed the hollow of her throat and moved down. He made it to her bra. With a firm tug, he revealed her breasts. She cried out when he took a nipple into his mouth, flicking his tongue over the hard point.

She'd never thought she could come with nipple play alone, but she was so excited she thought she might be able to. She increased the friction between her thighs, rolling her hips, riding the hardness resting against her pussy.

"Jesus, woman," he rasped, focusing his attention on her other breast. "You've really missed me like this, haven't you?"

"Do you even have to ask?" She didn't stop moving, feeling a warm rush in her abdomen. Just a little bit more, and she'd fall apart. Grasping his ass, showing him how she wanted him to move, she whispered, "Oh, God. Oh, please."

"Damn, you're hotter than hell." He slid his hand between them and rubbed his fingers against her jeans, thrusting his hand back and forth. Her breath caught, and he groaned. He moved away, applying more delicious pressure. "That's it, baby. I want to see your face when it happens. Come for me."

Between the hoarseness in his voice and his skillful fingers, she shattered immediately, thrashing beneath him. He watched her just like he said he would, a wicked gleam in his eyes. Her lids drifted closed, and she floated in the sensations, riding them as long she could, trying to steady her breathing.

"Hold on to me. We're taking this somewhere I can really enjoy you."

He lifted her, carried her to the bedroom, and placed her on the soft mattress. When he tried to move back, she held on tight, keeping her arms and legs around him. "Where do you think you're going?"

"You'll see, sassy." He patted her ass and slid out of her grasp.

She opened her eyes and tossed her arms over her head, watching him as he went into the closet. He came out with a small box. While the object in his hands made her curious, the devilish grin on his face had her blood pumping. He was up to something, and she couldn't wait to see what he had in store.

"What've you got there?"

"I already told you." He put it on the bed and reached to remove her jeans. "You'll see."

Damn.

It was official.

He was going to drive her crazy.

Kamden removed Everly's clothing, taking his time, appreciating the lean curves of her body. He let his fingers drift over her stomach and thighs. Her pale skin was soft and rosy, her nipples and pussy a cock-rocking shade of pink. She reached for his jeans, wanting to do the same for him, but he stopped her. She'd get at his cock soon enough.

"Not yet, baby."

He had two things for her, and this was the first. He'd known she'd been in a constant state of arousal, but he hadn't realized just how much she wanted him like this. Poor thing had come apart with a little bit of petting and nipple play.

Her response to him was the damnedest thing he'd ever seen.

Since he'd put her in the center of the bed, he had plenty of room to work. He inched between her legs, his gaze resting on her pussy. She was swollen and wet. He reached for the vibrator he'd gotten her, pulling it from the box. She saw it, and her lips parted, her lovely hazel eyes growing wide. He thought it best to start small and work his way up, not wanting to overwhelm her with toys that might seem like too much.

"Don't tell me you've never used one of these."

"I have, but..." He arched a brow, curious as to what

the problem was, and she said, "I've never had someone use one on me."

"I'm the first?" He slid the tip against her labia, getting it wet with her juices, slipping it up and down her folds. When she nodded, he told her, "Here's what I'm going to do. I'm going to slide this inside you, turn it on, and then I'm going to down on you. I want you crazy and loud. I want to feel your hands in my hair as you say my name over and over again."

When it hit her that he meant it, she whispered, "Oh, shit."

"Get comfortable, Everly." He wasn't stopping until she couldn't move. "I'm going to be here awhile."

There was no need to rush, so he didn't. He teased her for several seconds, rubbing the vibrator up and down. She lifted her hips, thrusting against him. He eased it into her, watching her pussy slowly accept the device. Fuck, what a sight, enough to make the base of his spine tingle as his balls tightened. His cock felt like it could pound nails, and he felt it jerk and pulse. Fluid seeped from the tip, wetting his boxers, seeping into the thin cotton.

Her whimpers had him changing things up.

He turned the vibrator on, got between her out-stretched thighs, and lowered his head. He'd been waiting so long for another taste of her. Now that he was face to cunt, he was going to enjoy it. He parted her with his thumbs and licked and nibbled, waggling his head. She was so wet she was drowning him, her cries music to his ears. She'd listened earlier, planting her fingers in his hair, giving the strands tugs and twists.

"Kamden." She writhed and groaned. "*Kamden*."

Her fingers clasped his head, her nails digging into his scalp. Her breathing changed, her inhales and exhales ragged and harsh. She was close again, almost there. Shifting up, he sucked her clit into his mouth. He had to put one hand on her stomach to keep her in place as she came a second time, her thighs flexing as she wriggled and squirmed. He didn't pull away when the orgasm passed and she relaxed, wanting to give her another one.

"What are you doing? I'm so sensitive now." She sounded like she was stuck between pleasure and pain. He let her figure it out, staying where he was, starting all over again. "Oh, God."

It would take longer this time, not that he gave a shit.

He worked her up, being more aggressive, using more pressure with his mouth, lips, and tongue. He brought her back to the pinnacle, kept her there, and didn't stop until she screamed his name. Her legs were trembling, and so were her hands. He shut off the vibrator and removed it, giving her a short reprieve. As it eased from her, he pressed kisses to each of her thighs.

"I'm going to run you a bath." He nipped her leg and soothed the sting with his tongue. "After I get you nice and clean, I'm bringing you back to bed and doing this all over again."

She peered down at him, looking a whole lot happy.

Just the way he liked her.

"Are you trying to kill me?"

"You think this can kill you, do you?"

"I think you wouldn't mind finding out."

My sexy little smart-ass. "You're right. I wouldn't."

He eased off the bed, going to do exactly what he said. He pulled out towels, filled the tub, and got everything ready for her. He'd gotten several items a few days earlier, wanting to make her time at his place more comfortable. He had to reach down and adjust himself before he went back to her. His cock and sac felt like they were going to burst.

She wasn't the only one eager for tomorrow.

So the fuck was he.

He went back for her, smiling when he saw she'd stayed exactly as he'd left her. Her head turned, their eyes met, and a satisfied grin appeared on her face. He took care as he lifted her, happy to see her ankle appeared completely healed. She ditched the boot soon, and he couldn't wait to take her hiking. She'd talked about it numerous times, lamenting her inability to take Baloo out and enjoy the nicer weather.

She giggled as he lowered her into the tub. "Bubbles too?"

"All for you, baby. You like?"

"Oh yeah." She sank into the water with a moan and looked at him. "You going to join me?"

He hoped she'd ask. "If you want me to."

"I want you to."

"Then I'll be right back."

Time for the second gift, one that would make or break things. He went into the bedroom, collected it, and kept it hidden as he went back, stripped off his clothes, and motioned her to inch forward so he could ease in behind her. When her slick backside brushed his cock, he tried to focus on anything but how good she felt against him.

She sighed, placing her head against his chest. "This is nice."

He hoped it was more than that. "Do you like it here, darlin'?"

"A sexy man. A beautiful home." She laughed and grasped his arm. "What's not to like?"

"I have something for you."

"Hmm?" She titled her head to look into his face. "Another surprise?"

He reached for her wrist, turned her fingers up, and placed a key in her hand. She frowned, looking at it, and her curious gaze rested on his face. "What's this?"

"A key."

"I see that." She grinned, flipping it over. "What's it to?"

"My house."

"What?" She moved away and turned so they could face each other. "You're giving me a key to your home?"

"We've spent every night together for over a week. We've spent every single day together for the last two. I don't want that to change, and I hope you don't either." He couldn't read her, and it worried him. Maybe he'd gotten the wrong message, seeing signals that weren't there. He figured it was time to reveal what Brady had told him. "I know you're thinking about selling your house. That's your decision, but I don't want you to go. I want you to stay."

"You knew?" He nodded, and she whispered, "For how long?"

"Since we sat down and agreed to get to know each other."

"You didn't say anything."

"I was waiting for you to tell me." She'd had plenty of opportunities when they worked on her place. He'd waited for her to bring it up, but so far, she hadn't mentioned it. "I thought you would when you were ready."

"I don't know what I want to do. I haven't decided yet." Placing a hand on his chest, she said, "It was wrong to keep that to myself. I should have told you. I worried if I brought it up, it would put pressure on you, and I didn't want that." She appeared uncertain like she thought she'd done something wrong. "We should have talked about it."

Reassure her, fuckhead.

"It isn't important. Not if you decide to put that key on your chain and move your things here. I want you to stay," he repeated, placing his hands on either side of her face, leaning toward her. "I want you to live with me, Everly."

The clouds parted, and he recognized the awe in her stare. "You do?"

"Fuck, yes, I do." It was time to tell her. If she didn't

feel the same way, he'd have to accept it. "If you don't know how I feel about you by now, you never will. I love you, darlin." Her eyes darkened, and he brushed his nose against hers, maintaining a level stare. "I love the ever-loving hell out of you."

Her lashes fluttered, and her lips trembled. "You love me?"

And then some. "More than anything."

She absorbed the words. Taking a moment. "I love you, too."

Thank fucking God.

He couldn't prevent the grin that spread over his face. "Just remember who said it first." He kissed her, keeping things slow, basking in her taste, feel, and scent. As he pulled back, he asked, "So are you going to do it? Will you move in with me?"

"On one condition," she rasped, looking at his lips.

If he could, he'd give her anything in his power. "Name it."

"I don't want to wait anymore. I want you and me to happen now. We have plenty of tomorrows to look forward to."

He couldn't wait for each one. "I'm all yours."

She came at him like a crazed thing, splashing water all over the place, sending waves of it to the floor. Snaking her arms around his neck, she pressed her mouth to his. There wasn't anything nice, polite, or gentle about it. Her tongue darted into his mouth, found his, and twirled around it.

Fucking hell.

She went to her knees, parted her thighs, and straddled him. There wasn't any need to get him ready. He stayed that way when she was anywhere near him.

There was no preamble or warm-up.

She grasped his cock, angled up, and slid her pussy down the length of his cock. The fit was as tight as ever, forcing her to work her way down. It felt better than anything ever had, her hot pussy swallowing him whole. The walls of her sex fisted his dick as she took all of him. She'd forgotten something important. They'd talked about marriage and children, but he knew neither of them was ready for that yet. Even if he didn't want to stop, he had to get protection.

"I need to get a condom, baby." She flexed her vaginal muscles, and he groaned. "If I stay inside you like this, I'm going to come."

"I'm on the pill. I have been since I was seventeen." She didn't stop, planting her hands on his shoulders for leverage, grinding against him. She increased the pace, riding him faster. "I want you to come inside me. I want to know how it feels."

"Holy shit." He hadn't been bareback in a woman in over a decade. He tried to think of anything but her, not wanting to come like a horny kid with his first girl. He grasped her hips, digging his fingers into the soft flesh. "Fuck, you feel good. You have no idea how amazing this is."

"So do you. I've been waiting for this for so long." She snapped her hips, taking him deeper. "You're so hard."

"Damn, that's good." He was going to blow soon. Without a barrier between them, he felt every single curve and clasp of her pussy. Bringing his hand down, he stroked her clit. "Just like that. Move for me. Don't stop."

He felt her trembling and wrapped his fingers around her nape, bringing her lips to his. He caught her cry in his mouth, feeling her quicken around him. As she came, he allowed the zinging in his spine to unravel, pumping his hips and causing more water to spill around them, groaning as his muscles flexed and he jetted inside her. The orgasm went on and on, making him see fucking stars.

She sighed and collapsed against him, panting softly.

She brought her hands down and wrapped them around his waist. "Tell me you love me."

"I love you." Because she seemed conflicted, he kept going. "I'll tell you over and over if you want."

She exhaled, her breath warm against his chest. She pulled back, meeting his gaze. His heart spasmed when he saw the tears in them. "I love you too. I've never felt anything like this before. It scares me." He saw the worry in her eyes. "I don't want to lose you."

"Don't let it scare you, baby. You'll never lose me. We're doing this together, and I can't wait to see what comes next." He slid his hands around her face, cradling it. "I'll show you I'm worth it."

"I know you will," she said, rising up again to place her forehead to his. "Just like I'll show you."

"I'll hold you to that." He gave her a squeeze, wanting to get her off her knees. She couldn't wrap her ankles around his waist, and he didn't want to risk hurting her. "Let's move this back to the bedroom."

He shifted cautiously and moved around as he let her go. He didn't bother with himself, getting her out, making sure he gently toweled her off.

"You like this part, don't you?" she asked, stroking his head, combing her fingers through the strands on top.

"You mean taking care of you?" She gave a quick nod, and he warned, "Yes, I do, and I'll expect to do it every single time I can." There was more to it than that. "You take care of me too, sassy. You wash my clothes, clean up my messes, and feed me." He kissed her bellybutton and peered up at her. "You love me."

He didn't think anything could interrupt the bliss he felt until his phone rang. He'd programmed the ringtone on purpose, choosing The Imperial March to go along with the Darth Vader photo, wanting to know if a certain person called him. Since it was Saturday night, he wasn't surprised. Delaney had probably gone out, had a few drinks, and wanted to reach out with alcohol and courage in her system. He didn't know if it was serendipity or stupid fucking luck. He'd promised Everly she could handle this shit if and when it happened. He reached for his jeans, removed his cell, and handed it to her.

"It's the bitch," he said quietly, wishing it had happened at any other time.

Her large and expressive multicolored irises sparked, and she answered right away, "I'll keep this simple. I love him, and he loves me. Don't call again. Kamden's mine now, so fuck off." She ended the call without listening for a response, handing it back to him. "Block her and take me back to bed."

How could he possibly say no?

He did exactly that, severing the final cords holding him to his past, blocking the number and tossing his phone on the bathroom counter. He wrapped his arms around her, nuzzling her head, carrying her back to the bedroom. As he lowered her to the mattress, studying her beautiful face, he couldn't wait for tomorrow. There was a good chance he'd keep her up until the clock struck twelve and take her then.

Certain things in life made no sense.

But this wasn't one of them.

He wondered how in the hell he'd gotten so lucky.

EPILOGUE

"**S**TOP WORRYING, BABY." Kamden came over, giving her rump a hard smack, moving closer when he saw the doubt in her face. He smoothed the burn with his palm, cupping her ass, pressing his chest against her back. "You look perfect. Good enough to eat." He molded his sublime body against hers, meeting her gaze in the mirror. "This isn't a big deal, so stop thinking it is. You don't have to make anyone happy, just me."

She tried to accept that but struggled to.

He always knew when she needed more encouragement and provided it straight away. He glared at her, making it clear he wanted her trust and needed her to accept his words as he told her, "Everything will be fine. They already love you. You've got this."

She took a deep breath, studying herself in the mirror, wanting to be beautiful and perfect. His mother and father had only seen her in overalls and work clothes, looking nothing at all like she did now. She'd retrieved one of her prettier dresses, leaving her hair down. Somehow she didn't think it was enough, thinking she looked frumpy and stupid.

Since Kamden didn't want her in heels, worried about her ankle, she'd agreed to wear flats. It wasn't easy to admit, but she was as good as she was going to be, polished and pristine. Knowing that didn't help. Not really. She was about to face his mother and father, visiting them for the first time as the one who loved their son.

She wasn't sure what to expect.

"What if they change their minds about me?" They always could.

They could turn her away and destroy everything.

Despite the happiness they'd created in the last few weeks, she'd been consumed with self-doubt. She couldn't forget how things had been with her mother and father. She only had partial memories, all of them vague, of a time when her mother had stayed with her father. From those glimpses, she recalled happiness and laughter. But she couldn't remember, not clearly. A part of her wondered if they were real at all. If they were, she knew the score.

They'd loved each other once and things had turned to shit.

She knew Kamden would never hurt her. He wasn't the problem.

The issues arose from her own fears.

No matter how hard she tried, she couldn't prevent them.

She worried other threads in their lives could enter, corrupt, and ruin things that meant everything to her. Personal issues were a problem with couples but outside elements always added to them. She hated circumstances she couldn't control, afraid it would take what she loved from her. She'd gotten over losing her mother early in life, moving on, accepting that sometimes shit happens. Then she'd lost the only person in her world, forced to say goodbye to the man who raised her.

It had changed things, leaving her alone and vulnerable.

When she'd confessed all, telling Kamden she'd come to the house her great-grandparents had owned to stay safe, not wanting to let anyone else in that had the power to bare her soul and cause her harm, he'd understood. He'd built his own home in a different state far from Delaney, wanting to start over, doing pretty much the same.

Aware of her fear, wanting to eliminate it, he'd sat her down, and they had a long talk about everything that frightened them. They'd vowed to be open and honest with each other, meaning she had to tell him why she was so uncertain and afraid of things.

He'd held her as she'd told him her innermost secrets, stroking her hair and listening without interrupting. He was there for her no matter what, and he wanted to prove it. Kamden had a way of doing that, easing her concerns, overriding her fears. He combated the bad with the good, reminding her they'd come together because of the shitty things that had happened in their lives.

The man said he'd do anything for her.

And she believed him.

"They are not your mother or your father, and we're nothing like them. Not remotely similar." He rested his chin on her shoulder, holding her stare. "If anyone has a problem with this, then they'll have to get it over it. I'm not letting you go. I don't give a shit what anyone says or thinks. I'm keeping you, baby. You're staying with me."

The man wasn't lying.

After he'd brought her home a week prior and told her he loved her, he'd taken her to her house to get the things she would need at his place. When she'd asked if he was sure he wanted her in his home, he'd gotten on to her, reminding her his home was hers too now. It hadn't taken long, only a few trips, to bring everything to his house. Afterward, he'd used his crew to bring the things from storage she wanted, giving her free rein, letting her move and decorate to her heart's content.

She still didn't know what she'd do about the house she still had to finish, but he'd indicated she could take her time. She wasn't sure what to make of that, afraid of taking over his space, not wanting to take a step in the wrong direction.

"We're meeting your sister soon," he reminded her,

putting them on a level playing field. He did that when she worried about things, reminding her she wasn't alone. "If you can do this for me, I can do that for you."

Since he'd untangled himself from the clutches of his past, she'd decided to do the same. It wouldn't be easy, but she wanted a clean slate and fresh start when it came to him. She didn't want any lies or toxic family ties. She wanted everything out in the open, revealed to anyone and everyone.

The past had confined both of them.

She wouldn't let that continue.

"I guess I'm as ready as I'm going to be," she finally said, thinking her best wasn't good enough. This was the man she wanted to be with for the rest of her life. If his family didn't agree, it would be hell.

She knew about those kinds of things only too well.

"You're missing one thing," he said softly and reached into his pocket.

She wondered what he was up to and tried to spin around, but he kept her in place. He pulled something from his jeans and reached for her left hand. He made sure she was looking at him in the reflective glass before he spoke.

"I had this made for you." He lifted her hand, peered down, and slid a ring on her finger. "I wanted to get you something different, but I didn't want my family to overwhelm you. When they see it, they won't ask questions. You can be yourself and know what it means, because I'm about to tell you." He studied her in the glass, holding her gaze, his eyes brimming with love and adoration. "It might not look like it, but it's a promise ring, Everly."

Her breath caught, her heart threatening to explode.

"I promise that I will be here for you no matter what," he continued, resting one of his hands on her hip. "I'll love the hell out of you, watch over you, take care of you, and love you until you can't stand it. When the time comes, and you're ready, I'm going to replace it with something else that shows you how much you mean to me."

She broke eye contact, looking at the band on her finger.

It was a simple white gold band with pave diamonds. A thin dog bone rested in the center with Baloo engraved into the metal in cursive.

He knew the dog was her lifeline to the world. The canine was what she'd clung to on days when she didn't think she could make it. When she wanted to crash, find sleep, and forget about everything around her, Baloo reminded her she had other responsibilities. The dog had kept her going even when she hadn't wanted to.

"It's beautiful." She'd never take it off. She might move it to another hand if and when he replaced it like he said he would, but that single piece of jewelry would always be something important to her. "I love it."

"Are you sure?" He gazed at her, obviously wanting her approval. "I thought you might like something else, but I wasn't certain. I know how stressed you've been, and I didn't want to make things worse." He gave her an uncertain smile in the reflection. "I tried to be inventive. I wanted to give you something special."

He already had done that.

He'd given himself to her.

"It means the world to me. It's more special than you know."

He let her go then, turning her around, bringing them face-to-face. He slid his arms around her back, studying her with those bright amber eyes of his.

"Good, because that's what you mean to me." He tugged her closer, lowering his head, his voice thickening with emotion. "You are my world, Everly Mason. You are my everything."

Her eyes felt hot, tears coming on.

He was like this often, openly revealing how he felt about her, making sure there was no confusion. She'd never expected it, thinking he'd keep a part of himself from her. Yet he hadn't, wanting her as much as she wanted him.

She didn't want to imagine her life without him.

"You're mine too," she reminded him.

"I absolutely am. I think it's time we show the world, don't you?"

They came together, limbs entwined, arms hooked, embracing each other as they normally did. Like this, they weren't two people but a complete whole, brought together in a way she couldn't live without. They'd face everything together, taking on the world.

And she couldn't wait.

"I love you," she whispered, breathing him in. "I don't want to live without you."

"I'm glad to hear that, baby, because I feel the same way." His fingers drifted up her spine and tangled in her hair. Their eyes met, and he presented her with the grin that made her weak in the knees. "I love you, too."

At that moment, that truth was all that mattered.

He belonged to her, and she belonged to him.

Whatever came their way would have to face that. The man had given her a reason to believe. He'd given her a key to his heart and home. No matter what occurred, he'd given her something she couldn't deny.

He'd given her a reason to stay.

ABOUT THE AUTHOR

Aline Hunter has written stories featured in horror magazines, zombie romance anthologies, and flash fiction contests. Her work has a dark undertone, which she credits to her love of old horror films, tastes in music, and choices in reading, and has been described as "full of sensual promise," "gritty and sexy," and "a breath of fresh air."
You can visit her online at *www.alinehunter.com*

ALSO BY ALINE HUNTER

ALPHA & OMEGA
Salvation Mine
Immortal Mine

THE WOLF'S DEN
Sought

DESIRES OF THE OTHERWORLD
Wicked Deeds of a Warrior Prince

MAKE ME
Make Me Surrender